THE DANGEROUS WOMAN'S GUIDE TO DOMESTICITY

Book I: Exes and Errors

J.C. Smith

Copyright © 2018 J.C. Smith
All rights reserved.
ISBN: 1717840108
ISBN-13: 978-1717840103
First Edition 2018

Artwork by Elbetya

This is a work of fiction. All of the characters and events portrayed in this novel either are products of the author's imagination or are used fictitiously.

ACKNOWLEDGMENTS

To my husband, who loves me exactly the way I am; to my mother, who knew from the time I was four that I was destined to write; to my father, who taught me how to drive fast with the music turned up loud both on the highway and in life; to NJW, for whom I don't have the words to express my thanks; to Grandmother, who I have only recently discovered was a dangerous woman in her own way; and to my children, whose idea of me I can only hope to live up to:

Thank you. It has meant more than you can ever imagine.

THE DANGEROUS WOMAN'S GUIDE TO DOMESTICITY

Book I: Exes and Errors

1
COFFEE & WHISKEY

I NOTICED HIM AS SOON AS HE WALKED IN.

His sweater pooled at the top of jeans dyed a shade of indigo that made them look like they'd been struck through with velvet. Oddly, he wore brown leather slip-on sandals, as if this coffee run had been a last-minute decision. But it was his attitude that pulled the entire look together. He had an air of completely un-self-conscious cool. I watched him for a moment.

He looked around without taking his sunglasses off. I recognized that look. After a moment, he shifted his computer bag to the hand that held some loose papers and removed his glasses, scanning the room again. There was no chance of him finding a seat. Starbucks was packed.

I'll give him my table.

I surprised myself with that thought. But why shouldn't I give it to him? I was feeling friendly, and I liked his style. The nail salon wouldn't open until 10:00, and I was just killing time with my latte. Plus, I had a prime spot near a window and an outlet. There was little chance that any laptop-bearing coffee shop patron would say no.

I made the offer as he walked by, scouting for a table. "You can sit here, if you don't mind me finishing my coffee for a few minutes," I said.

He accepted and dropped his bag heavily in the seat across from me before stepping away to order.

Look at me. I'm a model Starbucks citizen.

I rested my elbows on the tiny table top and gazed out of the window, inhaling the aroma of my drink as it cooled in my cup. I ignored that my drink wasn't that hot anymore. Everything else about this moment just felt good. Sunlight poured over my face and shoulders. I slipped my eyes closed and enjoyed the warmth radiating through the window. I was feeling pretty satisfied with myself.

He sat down after having picked up his coffee. "Thank you for the seat."

"You're very welcome. Don't worry; I won't be here long."

I shifted, crossed my legs and turned my back to the window so that I wouldn't face him directly. It was a little strange to share such a small table with a stranger, and I had promised that I would leave soon. It felt right to create a little space between us. I gave him a polite smile and went back to my coffee.

"You are absolutely gorgeous," he said.

He spoke the compliment in a low voice, almost beneath the din of the coffee shop. I barely caught it. I leaned in, unsure of whether that was what he had actually said.

"Thank you."

I tried to keep it neutral, in case he had actually said

something like 'You just dribbled coffee down your shirt.' I checked my blouse as discreetly as I could.

"You really are. You're incredibly beautiful."

I heard it clearly that time. My stomach fluttered at the forward compliment from this handsome stranger. I let him see me blush, and he gave a little half-smile.

He was the gorgeous one. He was tawny with freckles and a smooth baritone voice. Something inside me stirred.

"Thanks. You just made my day," I lied.

The truth was that it was a few moments alone on a sunny morning, sipping the last of a coffee that someone else had prepared for me, that had made my day. This conversation was a gamble. And now I'd have to abandon my drink to hide my battered nails. It didn't matter. He was very easy on the eyes. I turned to face him directly, tucked my hands under my thighs, leaned forward and grinned.

He pulled out a flask and poured something into his coffee. That was naughty.

"Sorry," he said. "It's a little habit I picked up from my brother."

He didn't seem sorry at all. I had to laugh.

We slipped into conversation, almost without trying. He was a former banker who was now an amateur movie producer. He split his time between Los Angeles and Detroit, where he was caring for his mother. He was confident, easygoing and beautiful. I drank in his looks as we talked, and enjoyed the sudden awareness of blood coursing through my body. My cheeks warmed as he openly complimented me throughout our conversation.

"This is really cool," I said. I meant it.

He leaned back in his chair. "This *is* cool," he nodded.

"I mean, it's incredible to meet someone like this and just...connect so easily. I'm really enjoying this." I couldn't believe myself. I didn't want the conversation to end.

"I'm Lily," I said, extending my hand.

"Jonathan," he said. He grasped my hand in his and shook.

"Jonathan." I memorized the movement of my lips and tongue as I spoke his name. It's a little thing I do when I want to commit a name to memory. I'm awful when it comes to names.

He smiled faintly as he watched my lips move, and I checked at the sudden intimacy between us. His gaze met mine again and his eyes softened, almost imperceptibly.

"I'd better go," I lied. "You need to get started on your work, and I really need a manicure." I slipped my purse over my forearm and grabbed my almost-empty coffee cup with one hand, then fished for my keys with the other. It was all for show. I needed to break eye contact.

"I would like to see you again."

I didn't miss a beat. I had mentioned my husband and girls throughout the conversation, so I certainly wasn't hiding anything.

"We'd love to get to know you better. In fact, I'm sure that my husband would love to meet you. We both like meeting interesting people. I know that you travel a lot and that you'll be on the road next week, but give me a call the next time you're in town. We'll get some friends together and you can meet some other people who we find interesting."

I hated sounding so stiff, but I had to put some distance between us. My fingers found one of my cards as I chatted, and I handed it to Jonathan.

He was undeterred. He took the card, set it on the table

and grasped my hand with both is his. The world went silent for a long moment.

"I would go anywhere to see you again."

Damn. He just made me drop my keys.

As I stooped to pick them up, I realized that Jonathan could see down my blouse. I laughed a little. This is too rich. My eyes were still smiling when they met his, and I felt another little electric jolt.

It had been a long time since I'd felt anything like this. Jonathan really had just made my day.

I headed toward the door. *Don't turn around. If he's not watching, you'll look like an idiot. If he is watching....*

I looked over my shoulder. Jonathan had turned around in his seat and was watching me leave. I gave him a small smile as I pushed the door open.

...It'll look like an invitation.

I'm sure I didn't actually hold my breath all the way to the car, but it certainly felt that way. I exhaled deeply once I was in the driver's seat, grateful to be back in my own space. What had just happened? I was tingling from my scalp to my fingertips.

I pulled out of the parking lot and onto the road. The sky looked brighter; the cars like sharp metal cutouts against the asphalt road. I felt distinctly, madly alive.

My phone pinged. It was a text message. There was another ping. This was amazing! I had only been gone for one minute and he was already texting me. I decided to play it cool. I wouldn't touch my phone. After all, I was driving. Plus, I would need some time to pull myself together before texting him back.

Three minutes later, I had pulled into a parking spot at the nail salon. I took my phone out of my purse and stared at the sleeping screen. I felt so good. What if his messages turned out to be a letdown? I cringed at the thought of little gems like "Hope u r good" or "See you l8r". I wasn't ready to break the spell just yet.

I smiled through my manicure and pedicure, letting my thoughts wander. I had a lot to sort out. It had felt so good to meet Jonathan. It felt even better to know that the feeling had been mutual. What the heck was I even doing? I was a married woman living in suburbia. I couldn't just go around meeting gorgeous strangers at the local coffee shop. But it wasn't every day that I felt that kind of spark. The phone pinged one more time as I admired the sheer baby pink on my fingernails. I thanked my manicurist and made my way to the privacy of my car.

I slid into the driver's seat, pulled out my phone and opened my messages.

I slid into the driver's seat, pulled out my phone and opened my messages.

> •••○○ Sprint LTE 12:48 PM 61% ■
>
> ‹ Messages **ICE Aaron** Details
>
> What's up, sexy!
>
> You know I like those jeans you were wearing this morning. Why don't you come home so I can show you just how much I liked them....
>
> Tacos for dinner? We have ground beef and shells.

It was my husband.

* * *

My middle daughter, Morgan, came bounding into the kitchen. She had smudged maize and blue on her face, warrior-paint style. I had a bag of gourmet gummy bears on the counter next to me. I scooped up the bag with one hand, transferred it behind my back to the other hand and deposited it onto the seat next to me in one move. I didn't feel like sharing.

Morgan gave me a big, dimpled grin. I knew what was coming.

"Gooooooo Blue!" she bellowed. I watched as her pre-adolescent belly puffed, and flattened again as she pushed out the words.

I pretended not to understand what she had said. "I'm sorry; what was that?"

She sucked in another deep breath and her belly expanded like she had swallowed a small watermelon.

"Oh, wait. I heard you," I interrupted. "You said 'Go Blue.' Tell me, sweetheart, what is a Blue?"

Morgan's laugh tinkled like a rocky stream. "Mo-om," she slumped her shoulders in mock exasperation. "It's only the best D1 college football team ever. The best of the Big 10." She cocked her head and narrowed her eyes at me. "You know that." She shook her head, disappointed. "You really need to get with the program, mom. Football is life."

"Really? So, is that what's going on with your face right now? Life?"

Morgan paused as she looked at me. Her face broadened into a grin again. "Oh, yeah. I forgot about that."

"Well, thank you," I replied. "If it weren't for you, I wouldn't know anything at all about this thing called life. It turns out that it was about football the whole time. Now I can really live."

"You're welcome," she said, not missing a beat.

I wasn't a sports fan, but that didn't matter. It was impossible not to know that it was football season. The town was painted with University of Michigan maize and blue and Michigan State green and white. Locally-produced commercials for everything from carpet dealers to pet stores had managed a mention of college football. Husband-wife pairs that had attended the two different schools jokingly called themselves "mixed marriages."

"Wait a second. Where did you get that face paint?" I didn't have makeup colors that came close to the ones on her face, and it wasn't the kind of thing that Aaron would buy.

"Party favor from Cassie's," Morgan tossed over her shoulder as she bounded upstairs, skipping every other step.

I made a mental note to check the next favor bag that came home from a birthday party. People were as likely to send kids home with U of M face paint as with candy or noisemakers, and the birthday parties just kept coming.

I took a deep breath and put the gummy bears back on the counter. *Here we go again. Girl birthday party, age 6. Gift? Check. Wrapping paper? Check. Scissors? Tape? Sharpie? Check, check and check. Gummy bears? Check. Because it's 1pm and I'm going to lean on gummy bears to get me through this instead of whiskey.*

I smiled at that last thought. There was nothing to stop me from having a finger of whiskey to numb the experience of wrapping Girl Birthday Gift Number Nine of the school year. I just didn't want to ruin a good drink with another kid birthday present. It could wait until later.

One of the other moms had tipped me off that I could buy all kids' birthday gifts at one time. I had a stash of toys for the six-year-old set (Inanna's friends) and the ten-year-old set (Morgan's friends). I left it to Kali to choose her own friends' gifts, hoping that it would gain me some insight into the 15-year-old mind. So far, I had nothing. We usually ended up buying gift cards for them.

The unwrapped boxes were tucked away in two bins in the storage closet, each stocked with identical items. This little tip saved me from the dreaded last-minute birthday gift run. It didn't really matter that all of the girls got the same gift from our family. Ours were but one small part of a great circulatory system of kids' birthday presents that flowed through the families of our children's friends.

This was my favorite girl party wrapping paper. It was a tonal mix of purple camouflage, ranging from pale lavender to deep grape. I unrolled a length of wrapping paper and cut it with the scissors without measuring.

Ha! Ninth time's the charm!

That wasn't exactly true. I had wrapped the exact same gift three other times, not eight. The other four gifts had been for nine-year-old birthday girls. I rewarded myself with a few gummy bears.

I creased the corners and tucked and folded the scissor-cut edges of the paper into an even seam, lining it up and folding to tight, near-perfect corners. Wrapped with care, even a simple box of Legos could seem really special. I really enjoyed taking the time to wrap each gift with care. A beautifully-wrapped gift never disappoints.

Of course, that idea might be lost on a six-year-old kid who's hopped up on birthday cake and is on a gift-opening tear, but it wouldn't be lost on her mom. Presenting beautifully-wrapped gifts to kids was more than a nicety, it was a form of social currency. I could negotiate a playdate for my kid on my gift-wrapping skills alone, and I usually did.

I grabbed a few more gummy bears from the bag and checked my phone. It had been four days since I met Jonathan, and still there was no message from him. Of course he wasn't going to call. Why would I want that, anyway? I shook my head. The whole thing was impossible. I could hardly believe that I was still thinking about it. It felt silly, like a crush. I could count on one hand the number of people who made me feel giddy, and most of them were celebrities who I'd never actually met. I dismissed the thought and got back to work.

I measured a length of wide, primary yellow grosgrain ribbon, wrapping it around one length of the box, twisting it over itself on the underside and re-wrapping until the ends joined at the top side of the box. I left a generous amount for tying a bow and cut the ribbon. I knotted it, tied it into a bow and snipped the ends diagonally.

Now, it was time for Inanna to add the finishing touch. I called her into the kitchen. There was a long pause, then the sound of feet pounding the wood floors. Inanna ran into the room at top speed, holding the iPad in both hands. She stopped a couple of feet away and looked at me with impossibly large brown eyes.

"Yes, mom?"

I sighed. We had been through this so many times before.

"Inanna," I started pointedly. "I told you not to run with the iPad. You could hurt yourself really badly. And remember how you broke the last iPad?"

"Yes," she whispered. Her chin tucked in slightly and the corners her mouth pulled downward into a frown. Her eyes watered. She was the only person I knew who actually frowned when she was upset. It was kind of endearing. I couldn't help but go easy on her.

I leaned in close and whispered into her forehead. "Listen, baby doll. Just...try to remember."

I was so close that I could feel my own breath as it rebounded from her skin. I stayed there a moment and inhaled her scent. She was as tall as an eight-year-old, but still had that little-kid smell that I loved. I kissed the spot between her eyebrows. Her eyes brightened.

I stood up and presented her with an uncapped marker. "Please sign this card for your friend. Write your name at the bottom. Here." I pointed to a spot at the bottom of the card for her to write her name.

We had been through this routine for so many birthday parties that I thought she had finally gotten the hang of card-signing. She hadn't. The last time I left her alone to sign a card, she wrote her name at the top. I flipped out for just a moment before realizing that the birthday girl wouldn't care any more than she cared about my careful gift wrapping.

Inanna signed the card, the stem of the 'I' wobbling shakily; the final 'a' a shrunken circle with a stick that barely touched its right side. Looked fine to me. She wrote her friend's name on the front of the envelope, and drew a few numbers on it for good measure. Inanna was into number art lately. She often filled pages at a time with numbers written in vertical columns, and in different sizes and colors. I sealed the envelope and and tucked it under the bow. So pretty. Inanna agreed.

"Am I done now?" She was sweetly blunt.

"Yes, baby doll."

I couldn't help but smile at her. She was my youngest child, and even more than with my two older daughters, I recognized an echo of myself in her. Looking at her felt like looking at myself in miniature.

"OK." She turned to leave, then spun on her heel. I held my breath in anticipation of another iPad disaster. "Wait -- can you download this game for me? It's called Puppy Strike."

She thrust the iPad under my nose. This was the third game I had downloaded today.

"Thanks, mom."

She took the device out of my hands as soon as I had finished entering my password and ran down the hallway to the playroom, iPad clutched in both hands. I didn't bother reminding her not to run. Running was the only way she seemed to move from place to place.

I sighed and rummaged through the bag for a pineapple-flavored gummy bear. I had gotten the treats from a fancy candy shop that had them in hundreds of flavors. The girls had sampled nearly all of the candies, but I had stuck with an old favorite: gummy bears. I had chosen pineapple, watermelon, mango, grapefruit, Dreamsicle and banana creme. They were divine.

Dreamsicle and banana creme surprised me with their creamy yumminess, and I had eaten them the day before. They were soft and fresh, unlike anything I'd ever bought in a package. I only realized when the girls and I took our modest bags of novelty candy to the register that I had bought nearly $50 of sugar. I had thought about leaving the bags of candy at the counter, but we had had so much fun browsing the rainbow of confections and marveling at the novelty flavors. It would have been a real buzzkill to just abandon our haul. I sighed and handed over my credit card. The spotty teen behind the register barely acknowledged my resignation. He'd seen that look a thousand times before.

Now that the two most delicious flavors were gone, I moved on to my next favorite ones. I took two bears and turned them so that they were facing each other, then flipped one upside down so that they aligned in a 69 position. I watched as my two second-tier favorite flavors, a pale yellow pineapple and a pink champagne-colored grapefruit gummy bear bulged and squeezed between my thumb and forefinger, nuzzling each other's neutered crotches. I squished them together, first one end, then the other. I had enjoyed eating gummy bears like this for as long as I could remember. They joined together perfectly that way and it never failed to make me smile. Squish-bulge. Squish-bulge.

My phone pinged and my stomach flipped. I had been thinking about Jonathan for days -- had I finally conjured up a text from him? I popped both gummy bears in my mouth and grabbed the phone.

```
●●●●○ Sprint 🗢        2:14 PM         ● 83% ▰
    ‹ Messages      Juliana             Details

            ┌─────────────────────┐
            │ What's going on, pretty │
            │ lady?               │
            └─────────────────────┘
            ┌─────────────────────┐
            │ We haven't talked in a │
            │ while. Did you find a new │
            │ boyfriend?          │
            └─────────────────────┘




    📷   Text Message                  Send
```

I rolled my eyes and flipped my phone to Do Not Disturb mode so that we could text each other without drawing the interest of everyone in the house. I didn't really appreciate being teased like this. I fired off a reply:

> **Juliana:** What's going on, pretty lady?
>
> We haven't talked in a while. Did you find a new boyfriend?
>
> Oh, yeah. I have a new boyfriend. We stay up all night and talk and text, and sometimes we meet for hot sex in a hotel.
>
> Being married with three kids and a lover is just too boring for me. I thought I'd bring on another boyfriend just for kicks. You don't mind, do you?
>
> Now, ask me another crazy question.

Julian didn't know how close he had come to the truth. He had no idea about my encounter with Jonathan a few days before. I couldn't help feeling silly for hoping for a message from Jonathan. I had actually indulged in a crush on a man in a coffee shop.

Really, who has a husband and two boyfriends? I shook my head at the sheer recklessness of it. *Now, that would really be outrageous.*

I crossed the room and grabbed a lowball glass etched with a world map out of the cabinet. It was time for a glass of whiskey.

2.1

ENOUGH LOVE

HER FIVE-YEAR-OLD FINGERS SQUEAKED AGAINST the glass as she wrote each family member's name in the cold condensation on the inner surface of the window. She paused for a moment with her finger pressed against the glass. Warmth radiated from her fingertip, and the resulting clear spot bloomed into a blurry-edged oval.

"What's the baby's name again?" she asked.

Her little brother had just come home from the hospital. Her parents had waited until the last moment to name him. They had wanted to meet him first, just as they had with her.

Later, her mother would show her the list of names that could have been her own. She wrinkled her nose at the thought that her name could have been Ella or Athena or Marguerite; David or Marcus or Edward if she had been born a boy. Instead, they named her Lilith.

"I held you in my arms and I knew. I looked into your eyes, and even as an infant, they could pierce your soul. You had a full head of hair that was like a halo of soft curls, and little bow-shaped lips. Yes, you were my little Lilith, even then." Her mother had told her this story more times than she could count.

Lily had been concerned about her little brother's arrival. It had just been the three of them until now. Mommy, daddy and her. The universe of her family was complete. They didn't need a new body in this system.

"I want to show you something," her mother had said.

She rummaged through a kitchen drawer and produced a book of matches. Then, she stooped and grabbed a couple of candles from the lower cabinet, where they were stowed for fancy dinners and emergencies. Her mother believed in using the best of what she had for the family; not waiting for some future when "guests" may come. She would lay out elaborate place settings for Lily, and later for Lily's younger brother and sister. No special occasion was necessary.

Lily would not appreciate this until much later in life, when she had had her own children. In the meantime, she learned how to handle china and crystal and learned place settings on the modest dining room table in her parents' modest New Jersey house. Candles were always at the ready. In fact, the family was more likely to have an impromptu fancy family dinner at home that they were to have a power outage.

Her mother struck the match. The tip flared with a pop and a sizzle. Lily's brain was imprinted with the distinctive smell of phosphorus and potassium chlorate. It sucked in oxygen with a soft inhaling sound then flared into a flame that danced at the end of the match. Lily would later learn that this reaction mimics that of an even more volatile explosive called Armstrong's mixture.

Her mother lit the first candle. "This is the love that your father and I had for each other when we met. It burned hot and bright and beautiful. And this..."

She touched the wick of the second candle to the flame of the first. The new flame flared and burned bright; a twin to the first.

"...This represents our love for you when you were born. It burns as brightly as the first flame, but doesn't take anything away from it."

She searched the child's eyes for understanding. She set the second candle alongside the first in a candle holder. They watched the two flames for a few moments.

"And now that little Noah is here..." she continued, reaching for a third candle.

"Now that Noah is here, there's enough love for all of us," Lily piped up.

Her mother hugged Lily to her breast. The little girl could hear her mother's heartbeat. She could smell her skin. She was enveloped in the warmth of her mother's body.

"Yes, baby," her mother whispered into her daughter's braided hair. "There's enough love for all of us."

Years later, her parents' love had cooled to a simmering resentment. There had been enough love, all right. Enough for her mother, her father, all of the children and at least three other women. At least that was what she had pieced together from the white-hot arguments she overheard late at night when she and her brothers should have been sleeping.

The arguments alone wouldn't have been so bad. There was the one time that she had actually caught her father kissing another woman. It had broken something inside -- something as fine as crystal or china -- something that wasn't being saved for someone else, but was supposed to be there for her to use and enjoy.

As she bloomed with the inevitable beauty of sexual maturity, she would remember both the flame and its burn. Her parents' love had extinguished itself too quickly. She was looking for a controlled burn; one that had all of the light but not nearly as much heat.

2.2

LIKE SPRINGTIME

I checked the time on my phone again. It was still 4:16.

Oh my gosh. I'm actually nervous.

I willed my heartbeat to slow. I sucked in a deep breath and held it for three seconds before I exhaled completely. My heart drummed in my chest, more slowly now, but just as loudly. I had only started counting the number of times I checked my phone since 4:10.

Don't be nervous. It's just a phone call.

I opened Pinterest and searched for "preteen girl birthday party ideas." The screen exploded with endless permutations of pink, purple, glitter, hashtags and exclamation points. I sighed heavily and forced myself to focus on the images on the screen.

My stomach lurched. What if he can't call at 4:30? My eyes flitted to the messages app as I flipped back to the home screen. He hadn't sent a text.

Maybe he sent an email.

I opened my email and barely flinched at the 216 messages

that waited for me there. It had been days since I'd opened my email app. I scanned the sender names for Julian Armstrong. Nothing. Who was I kidding? If he actually wanted me to get a message, he wouldn't bury it in that junkyard.

4:19. Eleven more minutes before Julian calls.

Just hearing his name in my own head made my stomach flip. I smiled to myself. That flutter in my stomach was butterflies. I was actually getting butterflies in anticipation of his call. I rubbed my damp palms together, then rubbed them on my jeans. My pulse picked up again.

No big deal. It's just a conversation with the one that got away. I'm sure there are a thousand other couples reuniting across the world, right at this moment. Thanks, Facebook.

Just as soon as I had the thought, I reminded myself that I was the one who had gotten away. It was impossible to keep count of the number of times that we had broken up and gotten back together. I had technically broken up with him the very last time -- or, rather, I had not accepted him back. We had left things unclear. In fact, we had never actually talked about it.

I had spent more than a decade trying to forget him. I had told myself that he had never loved me and that I was a stupid girl for wanting to be with him. I had doubled down on the lie with a full frontal assault on my memory of our relationship. I had worked hard to erase the markers of his presence in my life, starting with his birthday. I'd transposed the date -- was it June 7th or July 6th? 6/7 or 7/6? -- and had rejoiced that I could deliberately confound it in my own mind.

The passing years smoothed out the sadness that visited me every year. I had wrapped the memory of us in layer after layer of scar tissue until it was little more than a lump in my consciousness. I could rub it and try to remember the pain of our failed attempt at love, but I had healed and moved on.

At least that's what I thought. When he first reached out to me on Facebook, I turned into a ball of bashful joy wrapped in doubt and sadness. I was infatuated again. Our Facebook messages evolved to text messages, and quickly moved on to furtive phone calls made late at night, or during stolen moments when we could escape prying ears.

He told me that he'd really messed up, and was stupid to have pushed me away when he should have held me closer. "I have never felt anything like I felt when I was with you," he had confessed. "Now that I know you're married, it just feels like someone else is with my woman."

I had felt a thrill at those words. He had called me *his woman*. Still. It was enough to energize me. I replayed his voice in my head, and the words "my woman" gave me sustenance for months afterward. The thought would overtake me unexpectedly while pumping gas or washing dishes or doing laundry. His words would pop into my mind as I put my makeup on in the morning, making me blush at my own gaze in the mirror. How was it possible that this person from my past could make me feel like a teenager again?

4:28.

There was no way that I could squeeze myself down the Pinterest rabbit hole. I closed the app and checked my power level, silently reproaching myself for wasting precious battery life. I wasn't even sure I actually saw the images as I scrolled through them. I sighed again, trying to slow my thrumming pulse.

You care about this too much. The phone will never ring if you keep checking it.

I slid the phone into my back pocket and tried to ignore it, then fidgeted with a box of matches on the table. Anything to keep my hands away from my phone.

Moments after I picked up the matchbox, my phone vibrated against my body. I startled and nearly jumped from my seat.

Call from Julian Armstrong. 4:29.

I couldn't help a smile when I saw his name on the caller ID. I'd have to change that contact name.

"Hi," I answered. I hoped I didn't sound as giddy as I felt.

"Hey," he replied. He must have heard the smile in my voice. "It's good to hear your voice," he said. "You always sound so warm and so..." his tone softened. "I just really enjoy hearing your voice."

He was sweetly redundant, and was clearly holding back. I was thrilled. He seemed as tentative as I was. We were both excited to reconnect, but nervous about revealing too much as we got to know one another again. I was oddly comforted by the tension. I felt so vulnerable, and it seemed that he felt the same way. We were equally exposed, reduced to our younger selves again, caught in a tangle of feelings.

We chatted about the weather and about what had happened in our lives since the last time we talked. As with our previous conversations, I felt less and less nervous as we chatted.

Maybe we can just be friends. Maybe I'm getting excited for no real reason.

I was sure that I was lying to myself again. If we were just friends, why did I arrange this call for a time when Aaron would be away with the girls? I shook off the thought.

We're friends. Just friends. Friends who make each other giddy.

I was content to let Julian talk about himself. I loved hearing his voice, but I was worried that I had become little too interested. I needed him to be the bad guy that I had imagined him to be for all those years. So, I decided to let him talk. At some point, I was sure, he'd hand me the proof that he was someone who I shouldn't be with. It was a weak plan, but it was all I had. But today, unexpectedly, Julian turned the conversation around.

"I want to know everything about you," he started.

"Everything?" I laughed. "Okay, well, my name is Lily. I'm 41 and I'm a Capricorn. I like sunsets and long walks on the beach."

"Not that," he countered.

"Well, what do you want to know?" I asked as lightly as I could.

"Everything. Like, how did you get to be you?"

I thought about it for a moment. "I don't know how to answer that question."

Even if I wanted to answer, I wouldn't know where to start. It was possibly the biggest question that one person could ask about another.

"Okay. Let's start with this: Who did you date after we broke up?"

"Ah, I see." He had gotten to the heart of the question. "You want to know my body count."

There was no way I was going to tell him that. I hadn't ever revealed it to anyone. But if he wanted a couple of stories, I didn't mind sharing.

I started with a story about the banker I dated while I was

still in college. He was nice, and his busy schedule worked just fine with my school schedule. I slept with him just once, and that was when I discovered that he had a body hair situation that I just couldn't get over. I had wanted to vomit, but we were so far along and I didn't want to offend. Julian hooted at that one, so I went on.

I told him about the construction company owner who I had met while I was running. We liked to run together, and he introduced me to otoro sashimi. He had an amazing house and would cook dinner at his place most evenings when I saw him. I remembered that he had great taste in wine. I slept with him, but always refused to spend the night, even when he begged me to stay. One evening he told me that his father would "flip out" if he knew that we were dating. He was talking about my skin color. I responded that my dad might not be too thrilled to meet him, either. From that moment on, he pressed to meet my father. I didn't want that. He insisted. It became the central tension in our relationship.

"He was really into you," Julian concluded.

"That's funny; I hadn't really considered it," I mused. "He was actually kind of a jerk. And he was mean to his dog."

"Why did you keep dating him, then?"

"Well, we had a good...a good physical connection." It was embarrassing to admit that to Julian.

He groaned. "Okay, that's enough. I don't want to hear any more about Mr. Construction Company and your 'physical connection'."

"Well, you asked."

He shouldn't have asked for stories that he wasn't ready to hear. It was precisely the reason why I hadn't asked him any questions about his dating past, or about his wife. I feared that hearing details about Julian with someone else would take my breath away.

"You're just a heartbreaker, aren't you?" he accused.

I couldn't believe what I was hearing. "What?" I gasped. "What are you talking about?"

"You just go through life, making these poor guys fall at your feet, then you break up with them for no reason. They just don't know what to do. All we want to do is please you, and you just break our hearts."

This was clearly a false rant, but I suspected that it contained his thoughts about our time together. He continued. "I mean, who doesn't have body hair?"

"Um, it was a three-piece suit. Made of hair." I interjected.

Julian giggled. "So, he had a little more hair than most guys. He couldn't help that! And you just left him with no explanation. He's probably still in his apartment now, crying his eyes out."

"You aren't here to see it, so I'll tell you: I just rolled my eyes," I replied.

Julian was undeterred. "And the poor construction guy. He was in love with you. He wanted to meet your parents. You just tossed him aside because of his racist dad. You held his racist dad against him?"

"Don't forget about the dog." I wasn't giving any ground.

"Right. The dog," he mocked.

"Hey, that counts for something," I said. "But let's go back to that heartbreaker comment. As I recall, it was *you* who broke *my* heart."

There. I had said it. I continued, tentatively. "It was so

hard...I still can't believe you you ended up with anyone besides me." I couldn't believe that I was exposing myself like this.

I swallowed hard. "And, well, since we're sharing, tell me more." I closed my eyes and said the words. "Tell me about your wife." It felt like I was asking my executioner to shoot.

He stalled. "I don't know...I mean, she's smart; she's an excellent mother. An excellent mother."

I felt a stab of jealousy.

"And...well, she's really girly."

What the heck does girly mean? Was I not girly enough for him?

I wasn't really ready to learn more, but I felt compelled to ask.

"So, how did you meet her?"

I tried to make my voice sound neutral. The words felt hollow as they came out of my mouth.

"Well, remember the last time I saw you?" he asked.

"It was when I had that apartment on Annette Street," I answered.

Julian described the last time we saw each other. The awkward meeting; the attraction that crackled between us; his attempt at a kiss that I had wanted but didn't let happen. He remembered it as vividly as I did.

"I remember thinking that you were finally over me," he concluded. "It was clear that you had moved on."

That couldn't have been farther from the truth. I remembered that moment. I couldn't let that kiss happen. I hadn't seen him in years, and he had tried to get intimate without even acknowledging what had driven us apart. Sex was always his way in, and I had always taken him back. If I had kissed him, I would have found myself back in the same cycle. The part of me that recognized the pattern of our relationship saw that moment as my greatest triumph. The part that was still attached to him saw it as my greatest regret.

"A little while after that," he continued, "one of my buddies invited me to a party. It was at Jessica's house. She was hosting. And, you know, we started dating."

"Wait a second," I interrupted. "Those two events have nothing to do with each other. You and me failing to get together has absolutely nothing do you with how you met your wife."

"Okay, okay. The two have nothing to do with each other." His tone was sardonic.

"Why'd you have to say it that way?" I asked.

"Never mind. Forget that I said anything about it."

I didn't pursue the point. If there was any connection between the last moment we had together and the way he met his wife, I didn't want to know about it. I changed the subject back to his job. It was safe, baggage-free conversational territory.

Julian had become a very successful entrepreneur, and had started a big-deal software company. I was proud of what he had achieved. But achievement had its drawbacks. He had focused almost exclusively on work for years, and had found that he had less and less in common with his childhood friends.

"Meeting new people is hard," he said. "I spend so much time at work that I don't really have time to meet people. And there's no way that I'd make any real friendships with people I work with. I mean, the tech world--" he broke off, trying to find the words. "Think about all the stories you've heard about people in Silicon Valley. People who will rip your throat out to beat you to market. In reality, it's twice as cutthroat as that."

"I get it," I replied.

I had spent my career in PR, and had seen plenty of bad behavior in the business world. "The incentives in your world make it such that people will do pretty much anything. I can see why it would be hard to make real friends."

"Yeah," he said. "That's part of why I want you in my life. You're one of the few people who knows the real me."

I had only heard him sound this vulnerable a handful of times.

"I really do understand what you mean," I sympathized.

When I met Aaron, I was doing well professionally and living a life that I loved. When we moved for his first cross-country assignment, my life was turned upside down. I had given birth to Kali just weeks before moving to Denver. In an instant, it seemed, my identity had been turned inside out. One moment, I was a young, childless professional surrounded by friends, family and a shining future. Even my pregnancy was kind of fabulous -- I wore four-inch heels until two weeks before Kali was born, and came to work the day before delivery to give a killer client presentation. I felt powerful. But just two weeks after she was born, I found myself in Denver with no family, no friends, no job and a newborn. Morgan was born in a small northern New Jersey town where Aaron had gotten another plum assignment. Inanna was born here, in the Detroit suburbs. I was three kids and three cities removed from the person I used to be. Even I barely recognized the person I once was.

"Do you know what it's like for people to know you for someone you don't think you actually are?" I heard my voice quaver as I asked the question. Julian had touched a nerve.

"No, I guess I don't," he replied in a quiet voice. "That

must be really hard."

"Yeah. Just like you, I really appreciate that you know the real me. Not me as Aaron's wife or me as the girls' mother. Just me."

We were both silent for a moment. I thought about whether to share more about what I felt. It felt like a risk, but he said he wanted to know everything about me. I took a deep breath and let the words tumble out before I had a chance to change my mind.

"Lately, I don't feel like I belong anywhere. It makes me feel empty. Maybe not empty, but...vague. Or something. I don't know how to describe it."

I immediately regretted speaking the words that I had thought for so long.

"Let's talk about something else," I urged.

I lit a match, enjoying the pop and sizzle as the tip ignited. I watched the flame dance for a bit before touching it to the wick of a candle on the table next to me. Julian was still silent. I didn't care. The silence was comforting. I stared idly as the flame bobbed and shimmied, its white light burning into my vision. I closed my eyes and followed the ghosted image of fuzzy yellow light as it drifted, disappeared and reappeared on the backs of my eyelids.

"I need to see you."

My eyes flew open. "What?" He had caught me by surprise.

"I need to see you," he repeated.

I held my breath. I didn't know what to say.

"I have a lot of gray hair," I finally blurted.

I was exaggerating. But it was very true that my body

wasn't that of the 19-year-old that he remembered. I'd had three babies since the last time he saw me. I passed my hand over the flame, closer and closer. I wondered if I had the nerve to pass my hand right through it.

"You're probably exaggerating. But even if it's true, you'll always be the most beautiful woman I've ever met," he replied.

"But..." I hesitated for a moment, then spit it out. "What if we get together and it's not as good as it used to be?" I grew bolder. "What if we have sex and it's...bad? What if...what if it turns out that we're just two pathetic mid-lifers groping and bumping against each other? That would kill me."

I pressed my palm as close as I dared to the flame, then clenched my fist against the burn on my palm. Julian was laughing by now. I laughed a little, too, lightly touching the burn with my fingertips.

"You have no idea how you make me feel," he confessed. "Of all the men you've dated, I'm sure that I'm the only one who's this into you. I mean, is it like this with Aaron?"

He paused as if he expected me to answer. I didn't.

"I know how it goes," he continued. "After a while, your husband stops paying attention to you."

That didn't describe my relationship at all. I didn't want to boast about how great my relationship with Aaron was, but I also refused to diminish it. Why did Julian want me to agree to some version of "nobody loves you like I do"? I certainly didn't expect the same from him. My feelings for him were as strong as they always had been, but I accepted the possibility that someone else loved him as much as I once had.

I chose my words carefully. "Actually, that's the opposite of my problem."

"Oh," he replied.

Silence.

I stared into the flame again until my eyes watered, contemplating what the hell I was doing. I didn't even try to imagine what Julian was thinking.

* * *

I was relaxing at home when I noticed my phone. I had put Julian in Do Not Disturb mode so that he could text me anytime without causing a disruption. He now showed up in my contacts as "Juliana." It was a flimsy disguise, but reasonably plausible. "Juliana" could have been any of the other moms at the girls' schools.

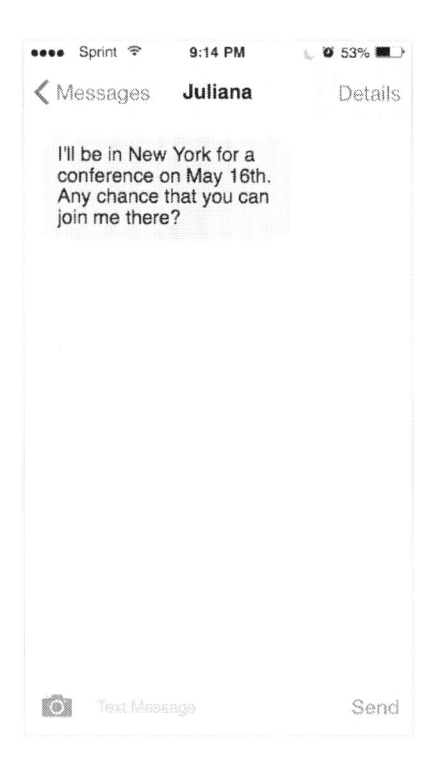

> •••• Sprint 🗢 9:14 PM 53% 🔋
>
> ‹ Messages **Juliana** Details
>
> I'll be in New York for a conference on May 16th. Any chance that you can join me there?

I panicked. I wanted to see him again, but was terrified. All at once, I was self-conscious and unsure of myself. I helped the girls get ready for bed, all my senses sharpened by the prospect of an actual meeting with Julian.

I checked my calendar. I still did some freelance work, and I had a client in New Jersey that I could hit up for work between now and then. So, yes, it was possible to meet Julian in New York. I'd make an excuse to be there on the 16th and 17th, then wrap things up early. I didn't want Julian to know that I was traveling just to meet him. It had to sound like I had other business.

I tried a few different replies to Julian's message, each more eager-sounding than the next. I had to strike the right tone so as not to over-sell our reunion, or to seem too excited myself. I wrote and re-wrote my reply, rearranging words and removing exclamation points. Finally, more than two hours later, I managed a reply:

> **Juliana:** I'll be in New York for a conference on May 16th. Any chance that you can join me there?
>
> **Me:** I have a client meeting in New Jersey on the 16th. I can join you that evening, once my meeting is over.

He responded in minutes, which nearly gave me a heart attack. Some part of me had wanted him to hesitate a bit. At least if I knew that he was nervous about this, I could feel better about my own jitters. But I was relieved to see that he was as full as nervous excitement as I was. I relaxed a bit, but still felt the need to lower his expectations for what he would see when we met. I no longer had the body that he remembered. I had to manage that situation.

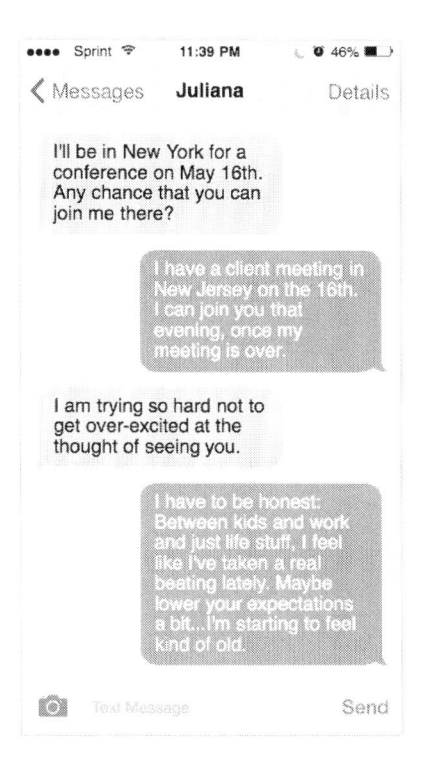

> **Juliana**
>
> I'll be in New York for a conference on May 16th. Any chance that you can join me there?
>
> > I have a client meeting in New Jersey on the 16th. I can join you that evening, once my meeting is over.
>
> I am trying so hard not to get over-excited at the thought of seeing you.
>
> > I have to be honest: Between kids and work and just life stuff, I feel like I've taken a real beating lately. Maybe lower your expectations a bit... I'm starting to feel kind of old.

I checked my phone for the next few minutes. There was no reply. My intent had been to lower his expectations, but now I was kind of mortified. Should I text him again and tell him that it's not that bad? No. That would be a disaster. I stayed up for another hour or so, pretending to watch TV. I compulsively checked for new messages. There was nothing.

My alarm went off at 6:00 the next morning. I still dimly hoped for a reply from Julian. Any reply. I reached for my phone and noticed a message indicator. There was a message from Julian.

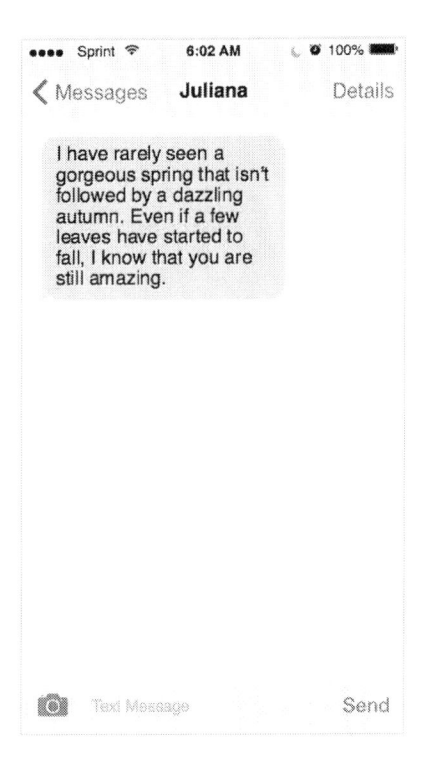

> **Juliana**
>
> I have rarely seen a gorgeous spring that isn't followed by a dazzling autumn. Even if a few leaves have started to fall, I know that you are still amazing.

I could hardly believe my eyes. Where had this side of Julian been when we were actually dating? I floated through the rest of my morning, flipping back to that message just to make sure that it was real; that I hadn't actually made it up.

It wasn't until that afternoon that I realized that I should probably reply. I managed a short response that expressed my joy at seeing his message and my excitement to see him again soon.

> Your message made me blush! You are too nice. I can't wait to see you next week.
>
> We're in a relationship. We don't have to be nice to each other anymore.

I tried hard to guess what he meant by that. Maybe it meant that his response was genuine, and that he wasn't just trying to flatter me. Still, I felt uneasy. I was beginning to think that we had two very different views of what it means to be in a relationship.

3.1

ON MOTHERHOOD AND KINK

Your BDSM Type:
92% Voyeur
84% Switch
81% Vanilla
68% Submissive
62% Exhibitionist
61% Experimentalist

"Thank you, Internet," Lily murmured, looking over her BDSM test results. She focused on the first six attributes, all of which she had been rated 50% or higher. She then reshuffled them, trying to draw down some kind of meaning, as if an online test could tell her things that she didn't already know about her predilections.

She had scored high for both voyeur and exhibitionist, with significant weight on voyeurism. Maybe they were two sides of the same coin. She smiled to herself as she replayed scenes of outdoor sex with an old boyfriend in a public park, and that one time at a party when she and her friends put on a girl-on-girl show for the entertainment of a small crowd. She silently thanked her lucky stars that her wildest days had happened before the age of cell phone video cameras.

Oddly, submissive and switch seemed like they belonged together. She thought about that one for a while. Maybe it meant that she was comfortable switching between being dominant and submissive, but preferred being submissive most of the time. That sounded right.

Vanilla and experimentalist. Did those make sense together? Lily had always joked that she was a try-sexual -- someone who's willing to try anything at least once. Something about that vanilla label rankled her, but she wasn't sure exactly what. She thought she knew what vanilla sex was. That couldn't possibly apply to her, could it?

She picked up her phone, opened a private search window and googled "BDSM Vanilla." Sure enough, there was a BDSM Wiki. A quick scan told her that "vanilla" seemed to be kind of a catchall term, reserved for people who weren't really into the BDSM lifestyle. That seemed to describe her well enough, but one section nagged at her:

> Attitudes and preferences associated with vanilla behavior include (1) distinct lack of desire for any kind of sex position other than missionary, (2) distinct discomfort talking about sex and other hot button topics (3) aversion to using sex toys (4) lack of conscious power exchange in relationship dynamics (5) fear or strong discomfort with content containing strong deviant overtones.

She couldn't believe that she had been labeled as sexually boring. She also couldn't believe that she felt the need to defend herself. Against whom? The great faceless "them" of the Internet?

She took a deep breath and went through the list, one point at a time.

Lack of desire for anything but missionary sex? Wrong. She smiled a little. That was easy. She felt a little better already.

She moved on to the next point: Discomfort talking about sex? She pursed her lips. Wrong again. What the hell, BDSM test?

Next point: Sex Toys. She cringed a little. She and an early boyfriend had tried using a few different sex toys. The problem was that they were young and broke, and didn't want to spend much of their hard-earned money on something they weren't sure they'd really be into. Lily couldn't help but cringe at the memory of the ragged plastic seam on the pair of cheap plastic anal beads they had tried. That was the first and last time she'd tried them. Then there was a succession of dildos and vibrators, each of which gave Lily the distinct feeling that a disembodied penis just wasn't as satisfying as the real thing. What she loved about men couldn't be reduced to a single body part. She loved the sound, the smells, the taste, and the feel of each one of her lovers.

It was true that she wasn't much into what they called a "power exchange." More men than she cared to remember had asked to tie her up during sex. She might have been willing to try it, but those men always seemed to ask that question too soon. It seemed too aggressive, and a bit scary. But maybe they were looking for the kind of woman who would say yes to that question too soon. She scanned the rest of the list. There it was. Rope bunny. The kind of girl who liked to be tied up. That one had come in low on her list at only 9%.

There was one last point on the list: Fear or strong discomfort with content containing strong deviant overtones. Lily shook her head. Wrong, wrong, wrong. She had looked at so much outrageous porn that she had begun to wonder if there was something wrong with her. Was she harboring some secret fantasy about suspension bondage, or violent blowjobs, or gang bangs? She had actually come across the BDSM test while watching some pretty violent porn.

It was a secret, guilty pleasure; not at all the kind of sexy stuff that she could recover from if she were caught watching. She had asked herself countless times why she looked at this stuff. And who were these women, anyway? They weren't really that different from her, she was sure. She watched those videos, fascinated. Each was like an alternative ending to a bad date that she'd had. Might that have been her enduring a face fucking if it weren't for the $50 she kept tucked in her bra strap for a taxi home?

She studied the women's faces while she watched. Some of them gave post-event interviews, like athletes fresh from the field of play. "Yeah, I loved it," they smiled through their streaked eye makeup. Lily wondered. She had been that girl, smiling through streaked makeup, lying to herself that it wasn't that bad; that she had tried it, and it was actually kind of good. She felt like she should have been outraged. Instead, she felt an uncomfortable shame at how the content aroused her.

There was some content that went too far, even for her taste: needle play, which was exactly what it sounded like, and breath control, which translated into suffocation for the person on the receiving end. And then there was something called figging, which involved inserting a piece of peeled raw ginger in the vagina or anus. The thought made her shiver.

Lily shook herself free from those thoughts. There were plenty of dark rabbit holes to get lost in on the Internet, and she didn't want to go down any of the scary ones today. She went back to the list of BDSM definitions she'd found.

"I just can't square this Vanilla label," she said out loud. "After all, I have kids."

She scanned the list. Tit torture? That sounded like breastfeeding. Scat play? She scoffed. Most people think it ends with diapers, but that can happen on any laundry day. Sadist? That's a mother of toddlers. Masochist/Painslut? Someone with a both teenager and a toddler. Obviously.

"Vanilla," she scoffed. "These guys don't know anything."

3.2

SWEET HOME

THE GIRLS HAD FINALLY SETTLED INTO BED. Aaron and I sat in the kitchen, spent. All the lights on the first level of the house were off except the ones over the kitchen island. Finally, we could talk about our planned kitchen rehab without interruption. We had been planning for months -- maybe years if you included the endless Google and Pinterest searches for just the right shade of paint, the perfect cabinet pulls, the ideal countertop color.

It had been a long day for both of us, and the girls had given us a run for our money that evening. But now, Morgan and Inanna were tucked in bed and Kali had showered and was finishing homework in her room. I poured a bit of Malbec for each of us, then raised my glass.

"To not letting the terrorists get us down," I said with a wink.

"Amen," he replied.

We sipped our drinks.

"I'm going to make some bruschetta before this wine catches up with me," I said, doing a quick step to the refrigerator to grab some tomatoes, basil, garlic and a lemon.

"Mmmm," said Aaron, rubbing his hands together. "I love it when you get me all liquored up, then make an extra sexy snack." He wiggled his eyebrows. "Makes me feel like you love me."

He reached over and fondled my hip as I walked past, pulling me to him. His knees were parted. I stood between them as he lightly squeezed my bottom.

"Liquored up?" I teased. "That's wine in your glass, Mr. Adams."

I pressed my lips against his, enjoying their pillow-soft warmth for a moment, then pulled away. He clenched his chest with his right hand for drama. "Girl, you're breaking my heart! Oh! My heart is broken."

I moved to the opposite side of the kitchen island, dumped the handful of foodstuffs on the counter and gave him a cool look. "That's not your heart," I said in my most sardonic tone. I raised an eyebrow and cast a meaningful look at his groin for effect. He howled dramatically, sending us both into giggles.

We chatted, eating bruschetta and sipping wine. As I took the last bite, I dropped a bit of bread to the floor. It was from the crispy end that I really like. I had intentionally saved it for last. Aaron was chatting away about whether we should replace or refinish the cabinets. Rather than interrupt over a bread crumble, I reached down, found the crumb and popped it in my mouth without missing a beat.

"And that's why I think we shouldn't worry about the cabinets," he said.

I was silent.

"What's wrong?" His tone quickly changed to one of

concern. "Are you okay?"

"Well," I started, "I was eating the last piece of bruschetta and dropped the really nice, crispy end." He nodded. He also liked the crispy ends and understood why this was important. "I picked it up and put it in my mouth, and, well, what went in my mouth was was definitely not the bread that I dropped."

He tittered. I could feel the corners of my mouth draw down into a frown. I couldn't help it.

"Ummm... was it a Cheerio?" he offered.

"No, it definitely wasn't a Cheerio. It definitely had a bread-like, crumb-like texture, but it was very sweet. Almost like a waffle."

We both sat for a moment, trying to remember the last time the girls had eaten waffles.

"I honestly can't remember --" he started.

"Nope, me neither," I finished. "Can't remember the last time we had waffles. Or pancakes."

The sweet, bread-like crumb had broken through my savory bruschetta and wine experience.

"You know, I'm not sure how to feel about the fact that I can't identify what I just ate. But really, I only have myself to blame for eating food off of the floor."

That did it. Aaron broke into a deep, open-mouthed laugh. I smiled sheepishly. He kept laughing, doubling over and grabbing his belly with one hand, slapping the countertop with the other. I started to laugh, too. He grabbed the bottle and poured a little more for me.

"Here. Wash down your...whatever that just was."

I shook my head, smiling, and lifted the glass to my lips.

***

Saturday.

I had just finished making brunch for Aaron and the girls, and had put the last of the dishes in the dishwasher. I had only had coffee, since I was going to lunch with my newest friend, Kelly. We had only met a few weeks before when our kids announced that they were best friends. Since then, our girls had had two play dates. I noticed early on that Kelly had a sharp sense of humor. We soon found ourselves arranging our own play date.

I couldn't believe it: I was having trouble deciding what to wear. I wanted to look good. I wanted my new friend to see me looking like myself, completely free of the influence of children. Kelly and I had seen each other in countless states of un-done-ness: Corralling kids and getting them to school in the mornings meant that most of the moms at the elementary school regularly showed up in yoga clothes, ponytails and baseball caps pulled low on their foreheads. I had talked to enough of them to know that many of us were un-showered by the time we dropped our children off in the morning. I'd even seen moms in pajama pants once or twice. Whenever I saw these women, harried and disheveled, I'd give them a little nod. Solidarity.

"Why are you dressing up?" Aaron leaned in the doorway, watching me.

"Am I dressed up? I don't really think so." I took another look in the mirror. "This one or the pink one?"

"That one." He nodded at the wool and leather sheath I was wearing. "I had forgotten that you're going on your lady-date."

I gave a short laugh. I liked the sound of that. A lady-date.

I took another look in the mirror and wrinkled my nose.

"Maybe I am a little dressed up. The only time I go out is when I drive the girls to and from school. I don't really go anywhere. I guess Kelly is going to get the gussied-up me."

I moved to the closet and pulled on my favorite high-heeled black boots, then finished off the look with a thin gold necklace and tiny gold earrings. I examined my reflection in the closet mirror. This was my look. I felt good.

Aaron slid behind me, hands on my waist. He craned down to kiss my neck just behind my ear. His breathing quickly synced with mine. Our eyes met in the mirror. He grasped my hips and bent me forward at the waist, then placed one hand on my back and pulled my panties down with the other. I smiled at him in the mirror as he ran his hands over my buttocks and down the backs of my thighs.

He disappeared, sitting on the floor between my legs. I could feel his hot breath on my vulva.

"Aaron," I protested, "the girls will hear us."

"Then you'll have to be quiet," he said, closing his lips around mine.

His tongue circled my clit for a few passes, then he settled in to work on my favorite spot. He passed his tongue over the top of it, back and forth in an upside-down U motion, completing a full circle or flicking his tongue over it intermittently. I had relaxed into him, but soon stiffened, hips moving almost imperceptibly.

He grabbed my hips again, fingers pressing into my flesh. He changed, sucking lightly. I moaned more broadly now. It felt like they were coming from a place beyond my vocal range, his tongue the key to their fathomless mystery. I was floating now, disconnected from my body. I could feel warmth climbing from the depths of my groin and into my lower belly. Aaron slipped a finger into me from behind.

My hips moved on their own, rolling with the waves building inside of me. I placed a hand on top of his head. My body stiffened suddenly, and I held my breath. Just as quickly, I reminded myself to keep breathing. I exhaled, then sucked in air deeply, pulling pleasure out of its secret depths. I imagined myself opening to to my man, a time-lapse of a flower blooming. The orgasm surged. I relaxed into it, letting its swell toss me where it would. I squeezed my eyes squeezed shut, mouth fixed in a silent howl. A dazzle of tiny fireworks burst on the backs of my eyelids.

My legs crumpled. I nearly fell on top of Aaron. I steadied myself on the dresser, leaning on my elbows. Aaron kept me upright, bracing my hips with his hands. His lips were still sealed to me, coaxing aftershocks from my body. As they subsided, he teased me with quick licks.

"No more...no, please..." I gasped.

My head pounded with pressure from holding in my screams. I was panting now, leaning forward on the dresser. Aaron stood up and wiped my juices from his lips with the back of his hand, then licked his fingers. He leaned in close.

"I love the way you taste," he said, letting his lips tickle my ear.

I blushed. After 16 years of marriage, he still found ways to make me blush.

He pushed his sweatpants below his hips, then swept my hair away from my neck with his right hand. His left arm wound around my waist. He buried his face in my hair near the nape.

"I love the way you smell," he murmured.

He buried himself in me, pausing for a long moment. I relaxed my body, adjusting to his girth. He started thrusting slowly, holding my shoulders and pulling me to him.

"Baby, you feel so good."

I tilted my hips, stroking him with each thrust. His breath grew ragged. Tenderly, he ran his fingers through my hair from back to front, stopping at the crown of my head, grabbing a fistful of hair. He pulled backward, exposing my throat. I watched us in the mirror, my back arched. I couldn't move. He grunted as his eyes met mine. His stroke deepened, slowed.

Looking down, he placed one hand on my hip and watched himself slide into me. He yanked my hair lightly, pulling me onto him.

"Look at it, baby," I coaxed. I could barely move, but I could still talk. "Do you like watching yourself slide into me?"

He responded with extra strong thrusts. I couldn't help a little moan.

"Damn, it looks so good...."

His body stiffened as he jerked my head backward and slammed into me. I could feel him throbbing as he climaxed. He moaned a little with each throb. It was enough to touch off a mini-aftershock me.

"Was that a..." he loosened his grip on my hair and stroked it lightly.

"Mmmhmm," I moaned.

We lay together for a few moments. I imagined that we made quite the post-coital picture: the two of us crumpled on a dresser top in the walk-in closet, him with his pants around his ankles and me with my dress around my waist. I turned, smiled and gave him a kiss. He pulled out and kissed my back from the top of my buttocks to the nape of my neck. My back arched softly with each touch of his lips.

I moved to the bathroom and grabbed a washcloth to clean up. After a few minutes, Aaron joined me, watching as I brushed my hair.

"I didn't want to mess up your hair, but then I realized that you hadn't done it yet. I hope I didn't do too much damage," he said.

He pretended to style my hair with exaggerated hand movements all around my head.

"You didn't. But you might do some damage if you keep doing what you're doing right now." I gave him a playful nudge. "See? Already under control." I had brushed it all back and put on a black leather headband.

He stepped back, appraising my look. "You do look really good."

"Thank you," I replied, then gave him a sideways look. "I have to go, so don't get any ideas."

My phone buzzed and I checked my screen.

"Oh, right. You get to take Inanna to a birthday party. It's at 2:00."

He groaned. "I forgot about that."

"So did I," I replied. "Thank goodness for my phone." I showed him my screen, with the reminder for a 6th birthday party. "I just do whatever it tells me to do."

"We'll have to get the girls out of the house so you don't have to hold back. I love the way you sound when you cum."

I blushed again. I didn't know what to say, so I pretended

not to hear him.

Damn, Aaron. You love doing this to me, don't you?

"You can act like you don't hear me if you want, but you know you wanted to scream when I licked your pussy."

Of course he had called my bluff on ignoring him. He could read me like a book.

This time, I recovered quickly. "I have no idea what you're talking about," I purred. "I'm a perfectly nice lady going on a lady date."

* * *

We were reading the Sunday newspaper and sipping hot chocolate on a brilliant, icy New Jersey morning when we got the call. It was a friend of Aaron's from grad school who had become a top executive at an automotive consulting company. He made an offer that was nearly impossible to refuse -- a three-year long consulting gig with Aaron as the lead. That three-year assignment rolled into a second, and then a third contract.

We moved to Red Oak Hills, a suburb about 25 minutes northwest of Detroit. It was a world apart from the from the tales of Detroit I had heard growing up in Chicago. Buffered from the wider economy by the auto industry, Red Oak Hills is part of a tight cluster of towns that seems immune to the typical metropolitan cycles of dying back and regrowth. Housing prices increase, at some times more slowly than others, but their value creeps ever upward. Hundred-year-old trees shade the streets during the day and stand sentinel over the unlit roads at night. Deer make their leggy trek through the backyards of stately homes, raising their babies in the safety of the miles-long ravine that divides one semi-wooded property from the next.

The people here have deep, nearly impenetrable social networks. Their ties often start from the earliest days of Mommy and Me and endure through adulthood. Parents create and nurture these ties like they would a grafted tree, binding their little saplings together until they grow into a unit. People who grow up playing together on a Little League team find themselves in the same fraternity at the University of Michigan or Michigan State, and later find themselves working for the same auto company in different capacities. They vacation "Up North" in lakeside cabins with extended family and childhood friends. They golf and fish and visit old mills and new wineries in idyllic villages with names like Interlochen, Alpena or Bear Lake.

Those who don't work for the automotive companies service them indirectly. They are the professional service providers like Aaron: the consultants, attorneys, tech workers, advertising executives and manufacturers whose lifeblood is the auto industry. There is the attendant constellation of professionals: the architects, doctors and accountants that attend to the bodies or the personal property of the residents. There are the med spa owners and gym owners and salon owners whose prosperity is built on their clients' quests for inner peace or outer beauty. There are restaurants and bars and upscale markets and farmers' markets, all with organic, locally-sourced delights to feed the bodies and delight the palates of its clientele.

Once, in an unguarded moment, I called the area a "big small town" to a local sales executive. He corrected me with a sniff: "No, it's a small *big* town," he puffed. I nodded as if this made sense to me, then made a mental note to keep any similar observations to myself.

What no one ever seemed to talk about was that this place is a graveyard for the careers of non-automotive spouses. For those of us who are transplanted here for a spouse's career, it can be a death blow for our own. Those with small children are caught between the limited outlets for of their professional offerings and the demands of raising children without the support of family.

These were people with varied and luminous backgrounds whose professional growth hit the same impasse when they move here. There was the former chef from Connecticut who now stays at home and makes endless versions of chili and casseroles to feed her three linebacker-sized boys. The opera singer from San Francisco who didn't perform for several years after her children were born, but now gets away for performances twice a year -- good for her! The former NBA cheerleader from Denver who has only now, after five years of raising children without much help from her husband, carved out time to take a nighttime dance class.

Besides a stunted career path, we all had motherhood in common. We were all doing our best to manage an unending rotation of dirty bottoms, dirty noses, dirty dishes and dirty clothes. We had each found ourselves, at some point, in shock at the transformation from the people we used to be to the people we were now.

The upside was that it made it easy to meet some of the locals. Having children had become an equalizing factor, reducing locals and transplants alike to a level of humility that most of us had never experienced before. We may not all have attended kindergarten together, but we could certainly identify with each others' challenges as moms. The local women I met ranged from a woman who inherited her father's manufacturing plant to a local

TV reporter to women who spent their careers as stay-at-home moms. These are the ones from whom I learned where to get my hair done and how to cheat my sagging brow with a strategically-placed hit of Botox from the right esthetician ("Go see Sherri. Oh my god, she's an *artist*.").

Kelly was one of a few good friends I had made. I had met her, like I'd met my other Red Oak Hills friends, through a play date. Inanna had become fast friends with Kelly's youngest daughter. As it turned out, Kelly had worked as an advertising executive before getting married, and had moved eight times to follow her husband's job assignments. She left her career 10 years before I did and was now a stay-at-home mom with six children. Kelly is the one who taught me that people like us are called "trailing spouses." It was perversely comforting to know that we had a name.

"Isn't it so different being at home?" Kelly wrinkled her nose at the word "different."

We were discussing one of our favorite topics over lunch: working outside the home versus staying at home to take care of children.

"Oh, my goodness, it really is."

I had been itching to talk to someone who wouldn't take sides on the whole working mom versus stay-at-home mom debate. My experience told me that it was a false divide. Everyone fails somehow, and no one feels like they're doing enough.

"To be honest, working in an office felt like it was all about me; about what I wanted professionally. Now that I'm at home, everything I do is for someone else. Even when the kids are away, it becomes about Aaron. For the first few months that I was at home, he genuinely hoped that I'd greet him at the front door naked."

"Jack did, too." Kelly speared some salad greens on her fork. "So now, I just use blow jobs to get what I want." She popped the forkful of salad into her mouth.

I was dumbfounded. "Don't you think that's kind of...transactional?"

"Transactional? Of course it's transactional!" Kelly replied. "Whenever I want something, I negotiate with my husband in blow jobs. I mean, our husbands have all the money, anyway. There was this coffee table I wanted, and Jack just refused to see why we had to buy that exact table. If it were up to him, he'd probably put a cardboard box in the middle of the living room and call it a day."

"Ugh, we're having that same problem with our kitchen remodel," I said. "We're doing this really modern look, but he insists on these horrible-looking cabinets. He says they look 'homey.' I say they look ugly. So here we are, stuck in planning mode."

"So you know what I mean!" She brightened. "I'm the one who has to live in that house all day long. He might as well be a visitor for all the travel he does. Anyway, I had finally convinced him that the table was absolutely necessary for the way we're decorating the house. But when he saw how much it cost, he nearly lost his mind. That's when I started negotiating."

I couldn't believe what I was hearing. Why hadn't I thought of that? I could have shut down that cabinet discussion weeks ago.

I quickly dismissed the thought. That just wasn't the way

our relationship worked. Until about a year ago, I had never had to ask Aaron for anything. I certainly felt the imbalance of power in our house now. Before, we had earned close to the same salary, and had split the household expenses. I had paid for childcare and school expenses. They were our largest expenditures by far. Ever since I stopped working, I have had to rely on Aaron for money. I had never had to lean on him so heavily before.

Kelly must have read the look on my face.

"Listen, I know what you must be thinking. But this is what we have to do. Heck, sometimes, I can't believe that this is my life. I have two master's degrees, and I'm using BJ's to get a freaking coffee table."

I wanted to laugh, but couldn't.

"I do know," I grumbled. "I have so little cash now, it's unbelievable. And on top of it all, I'm too embarrassed to ask Aaron for money. When I first started staying at home, he would give me money every time he got paid. Now, he forgets to give me money most of the time. I have to ask for it."

Kelly nodded sympathetically.

"And I really try...I go as long as I can without asking. Do you know how humiliating it is to have to ask your husband for gas money? It feels the same as when I had to ask my dad for allowance. I hate it." I felt a lump at the back of my throat.

It wasn't just asking for gas money that I hated. I had given up two of my favorite personal indulgences -- bikini waxes and manicures. Rather than ask for the cash, I had gone back to shaving and painting my own nails. Somehow, giving up those things hurt. I was ashamed to admit, even to my friend, how I mourned these minor extravagances. They were superficial, but they made me feel like my old self.

"Blow jobs," I nodded slowly. "They're like...a universal currency."

"Yup. Accepted everywhere," Kelly finished.

"I am so glad to be having lunch with you," I beamed.

We soon finished our salads. The server walked over with the check, and Kelly handed him a credit card before he could put the check holder on the table. She gave a wolfish grin.

"I'm buying lunch. Jack and I got into a huuuuuge fight last night, and I'm going to hit him where it hurts."

Kelly and I were enjoying each other's company. We didn't want our lady date to end. I suggested that we drive to the mall, where we could walk and talk. We chatted about the kids' school, our husbands and our houses. Soon, the conversation turned to our diets. Kelly had managed to stay tiny and fit through six pregnancies, but she had practically starved herself to maintain her figure. Now she watched helplessly as her oldest son, a varsity wrestler, went to extremes to make weight.

"I guess what makes it really hard is that I used to do the same thing," she admitted.

I sighed and shook my head. "So did I. I hate to say it. There was a time when I got through the day on nothing but Diet Coke and Skittles."

"I used to drink gallons of coffee and eat a single baked chicken breast with mustard each day," she added.

"Oh, so you were a healthy undereater," I teased.

She gave a wan smile and shook her head. "It was one thing to do that to my own body, but it's heartbreaking to watch my son starve himself. He looks really healthy, but I see how he eats." She paused. "It's like, where's the line?"

"Maybe when the season is over?" I offered. "I know that wrestling is important to him, but if it's not going to pay for college, he can stop trying to do things like make weight."

I hoped that I hadn't said too much. Her son was in love with the sport and was hoping to earn a scholarship. I was sure that Kelly had heard the comment. I was also pretty sure that she had just ignored it. Yes. I had said too much.

"Ooh, let's go there." Kelly pointed to the Louis Vuitton store across the way.

I nodded, grateful that she had changed the subject.

We were soon enveloped by the beiges and golds and honey blonde wood tones of the shop. I browsed idly, determined not to let myself love anything too much. Kelly, on the other hand, was on a mission. After a tour around the store, I joined her at a long glass counter where a sales associate had just presented her with a large bone-colored tote. Kelly slung it over her shoulder and turned to me, beaming.

"Did I mention that Jack and I got into a really *big* fight?" she said with a wink.

I widened my eyes in mock surprise. "No, you didn't! Exactly how big was it?"

She slid the bag off of her shoulder, held it in front of her and purred, "It was about this big."

Kelly handed her credit card to the sales associate and handed the bag over so that it could be boxed and bagged.

"Did you find anything?" she asked, turning to me.

"Well, I did see something I like, but..."

"Show me!" she insisted.

Kelly followed me to a rack on one of the walls. I picked up a blush-colored sheath dress in buttery paper-thin leather. It came with a matching Persian lamb jacket.

"That would be gorgeous on you," Kelly cooed. "You should try it on."

There was no way I was going to try it on. If I liked it, I'd only be reminded of my misery.

"Nope," I said, and discreetly angled the price tag toward her. It cost twice what she had just paid for her handbag.

"Oh, yeah," she concurred. "There aren't enough blow jobs in the world."

* * *

I couldn't get Julian's "girly" comment out of my head. I had googled it to find out what people say about it. The best I could come up with was that it describes someone who's very, very feminine. That wasn't helpful at all.

Aren't most women "feminine?" What does "very feminine" even mean? Someone who owns lots of pink things? Someone who likes to wear skirts? Or wait...is this a submissiveness thing?

I turned to Aaron. "Hey, would you use the word 'girly' to describe me?"

Aaron looked up from his phone, giving me a quizzical look. "Girly," he said. He seemed to turn the word over in his mind for a beat. "No."

"Right. I didn't think so. I don't think I'd call myself that, either."

"You," he stepped to me and pulled me to him, sliding his

hands over my hips, "are the sexiest woman I've ever met."

He planted a kiss just behind my ear and raked my earlobe with his teeth.

I pressed my bottom into him and enjoyed the feeling of his erection rising.

"That's what I'm talking about. See what you just did to me?" He stepped backward, arms spread, erection pressing through his jeans. "I'm just a victim."

I changed the subject. "So, what are we going to feed the girls tonight?" I cycled through our typical options. "Tacos? Too much work. Pasta with red sauce? Boring. Chicken and vegetable stir-fry? Wait, we had that the day before yesterday." I looked at Aaron for more suggestions.

He looked back at me and shrugged.

"It feels like there are only five meals that are easy to make and that all three girls will eat. I am honestly out of ideas. Should we just order a pizza?"

Aaron sighed. "Remember the dinner parties we used to throw? The amazing food that we cooked?"

"That was another life," I mused. "And I suspect that those were other people. People who I don't know anymore. All I cook now is chicken nuggets."

"Pan-seared salmon," he said, perking up. "We have a couple of large fillets in the freezer. They'll thaw in no time."

"Oh, good," I added. "We have asparagus in the refrigerator to go with it. And we can cook some rice."

Before long, we were moving around the kitchen together in a well-rehearsed dance, Aaron at the stove and me at the sink; fluidly weaving around each other as we prepared dinner. Aaron curled his arm around me from behind and kissed the back of my neck. Kali walked in just in time to catch the kiss.

"Okay, okay. Break it up, you two. Hey, what's for dinner?" She craned her neck and caught a glimpse of the salmon thawing in a bowl of water. "Oh, cool. I love salmon."

"Awwww, I don't want salmon!" Inanna's voice rang out as she ran down the hallway. "Can I have dinosaur chicken nuggets instead?"

I shot Aaron a look. Both Morgan and Kali loved salmon. Inanna's taste varied by the day, it seemed.

"Two out of three ain't bad," Aaron shrugged.

I put my hands up in a gesture of surrender.

I transferred the washed and trimmed asparagus to a bowl, drizzled it with olive oil, then seasoned it with salt and pepper. I grabbed a wooden spoon and tossed everything together, making sure that the asparagus spears were evenly coated. One spear flipped out of the bowl and onto the floor.

"Shoot," I muttered.

I stooped to pick it up. I'd have to wipe that spot well to make sure no one slipped on the olive oil.

"What happened?" Aaron asked.

"It's fine, I just dropped some asparagus."

Aaron didn't miss a beat. "Don't eat it!"

The girls all stopped to look at me. I held the piece of asparagus in the air for everyone to see, then dropped it into the garbage disposal.

Aaron had cracked himself up. He was nearly doubled over with laughter. As I moved past him to wipe the olive oil off of the floor, I gave him a playful bump with my hip.

"Shut up," I muttered. "It wasn't that funny."

That sent him into a new peal of laughter. Even I had to smile a bit as I wiped the floor.

4.1

WOLF IN SHEEP'S CLOTHING: A VIRGIN'S TALE

THE BASEMENT IN LILY'S HOUSE WAS UNFINISHED, with a concrete floor and exposed beams. So, her friend's basement, with its faux wood panelling and full bar, seemed fancy and taboo. It was clearly an adult space, and whoever tended it didn't expect the girls to discover the men's magazines stacked in a box in a corner behind the bar. The magazines had a powerful pull. She and her friend would sneak one or two at a time from the stash, then spend what felt like hours looking at them.

Even at eight years old, she understood that there were layers to what she was seeing. There were the women who posed with extra-short shorts and tops that skimmed the bottom curve of their breasts, or some with no tops at all, pretending at modesty with a well-positioned forearm. They were Ambers and Jennas posing as modern-day bathing Venuses caught in the act.

The magazines she studied most were racier. They showed fully naked women, laid across a bed or reclining on a rug. Their hair was long and impossibly big, splayed in coiled loops on the floor around them. Draped across chairs like luxurious dolls or bent over to show off their smooth flanks, they were all inviting something. They posed, arms open, knees slightly bent and crossed as if to point to the V at the top of their thighs.

She had never imagined that there could be such variety in the hair that they had down there. Curly or straight, barely-there or full-bush; each coif revealing much less than it concealed.

It would be another year before her breasts started to bud. She imagined herself with the full breasts that these women had. Those were the real wonder. That was what breasts were supposed to look like! Like everyone, she had seen them cloistered and fettered and all covered up, but she had no idea how glorious they could actually be. She made overly big, rounded breasts her goal. She could work on them, right? Just like working out. She wouldn't know until much, much later that nearly every girl her age had also read Judy Blume's work and worked the same mantra with pre-adolescent fervor: I must, I must, I must increase my bust! Results, of course, varied. Genetics was a bitch.

What she did know was that, even then, she had something in common with the women in those magazines. It was under the blonde or the black or the curly or the barely-there. It was was the stuff of fairies and witches; princesses and goddesses. A source of life and of soft, warm deaths. But somehow, that seemed better captured by the Ambers and Jennas who still left something to hide than by the Bambis and Bunnys and Cookies who hid nothing at all. It was with them that she dove into a study of comparative anatomy. She had examined their gynecology a full decade before figuring out that she could get a good look at her own with a hand mirror.

It was only once she got a good, long look at her own natural vulva as opposed to one that had its own attendants and makeup crew that she decided: Her vagina, along with her face, would always have some form of production value. Amber and Jenna and Bambi and Bunny and Cookie and what she saw in that mirror all coalesced into an image that would require a crew of a facialist, a personal trainer, a manicurist, the occasional masseuse and, of course, her bikini waxing aesthetician, whose level of familiarity with her intimate parts hovered just below that of her husband, and just above that of her gynecologist.

By 16, she had long since become expert at bringing herself pleasure. That summer, she graduated to the sweet, stupid boy who had hoped that cunnilingus would be the way to her heart. It wasn't. But it was a damn fine way to pass the time in an 8-week advanced studies program. Foxdale University was in the middle of nowhere. At least this gave her something to do besides study.

She had felt mildly bad about the situation, but she had been honest with him that she was not his girlfriend; that she liked him but probably wouldn't keep in touch after leaving the program. In the future, she would hear so many versions of his response that she would lose count: That can't be right. If you didn't like me / it / this / us, why did you spend the night with me / cum so hard / cum so often / smile when I said you're special? You say that you aren't ready for a relationship with me, but I know can change your mind. They never listened. They all thought they could change her mind.

He wrote several sweet, stupid letters when she returned home. She didn't call or write to him at all afterward. It was fine; she had told him that it would happen. After a few months, the letters tapered off and eventually stopped.

*　*　*

There was a homecoming party coming up. It would be hosted by St. Albans', the all-boys school on the southeast side of town. That was perfect. There was little chance of gossip spreading in the same way it might in a co-ed school; no chance at all of her prey having a girlfriend in school who could find out about their tryst.

He had to be socially palatable, but unlikely to cross her path outside of her planned encounter. And he had to have a decent body. Her current boyfriend played football, and was an incredible specimen of male peak fitness, even among his teammates. Kevin was 220 pounds of muscle packed onto 6 feet 2 inches of man that only happens with such natural perfection within a narrow band of youth and health.

She found her target. He didn't meet the same physical standard as her boyfriend, but that was fine. She wasn't interested in him for his physique. This was a surgical strike.

The condom smelled like a party balloon. It would become the sharpest memory she had of the event. And the sex? It just wasn't a big deal. It was supposed to be good, right? It felt so much better when she touched herself. But wasn't it supposed to hurt? It had only been mildly uncomfortable, but that could have been for any reason.

"Please. You're not a virgin," he scoffed afterward. He leaned back, zipping his pants as he cast her a side glance. "With your rabbit ass." She blinked at him. Rabbit. She had no idea what that meant. An image of Bunny was conjured from somewhere in the recesses of her memory. She pulled her jeans over her hips, laughing to herself. The deed was done.

*　*　*

She liked being at Kevin's house. It was almost always dim and smelled like men. He had three brothers who were much older. She didn't realize it then, but he was the accident child -- the one his parents had conceived when they were past the age they thought it possible. His parents were much older than hers and didn't like being disturbed. They usually stayed upstairs when she was over. It kind of reminded her of the adults in the old Charlie Brown cartoons. They would sometimes call down to him, yelling for him to take out the trash or run some random errand. They almost never made an appearance.

It was his brothers who had given him plenty of "education," about girls, if you could call it that. Kevin had been born 10 years after the youngest of them. The older brothers had made their fraternity the center of their social lives, and were eager for their baby brother to do the same. His brothers' mentorship aside, Kevin's physique, athleticism and social status had done plenty for him on their own. He had been with several girls at school, and had dated the lead cheerleader. It was practically a cliché.

But he was genuinely kind and sweet, and his popularity meant that his friends were hers, too: a lucky break for a junior year transfer student. He had walked her home from school every day for more than a year. She lived a mile East of their school, and he lived a little more than a mile West of it. It felt like a throwback to another time: the lettered varsity athlete walking his girl home from school through cold or heat or rain; the two of them sharing kisses at her house after school; never going farther than tender, fervent kissing.

The downside of his genuinely friendly and sweet nature was that all of the girls he'd been with continued in his orbit, including that pesky cheerleader. Lily would walk into math class to find her perched on his knee or whispering something in his ear, only to giggle and take a seat on his desk when she spotted Lily. As if that makes it any better, she had thought. And who the hell wears a cheerleading skirt in class? Why can't she change into her uniform later like a normal person? It felt like competition. She wasn't going to compete for her own boyfriend.

He had said that he wanted to marry her. She hadn't said anything of the sort in return, but she loved the fact that he loved her. The truth was that she was nervous and more than a bit intimidated. She really liked him. He had been so patient and had never, ever pressured her to go any farther than she was ready to do. But the real barrier was that he had so much experience and she had so little. She didn't want to be embarrassed when they finally had sex. She wanted it to be good; to enjoy it; and for him to enjoy it, too. She didn't want to be the ingenue. And she couldn't erase the image of that cheerleader bobbing on his knee.

And so, she had staked out the one who would help her move past being a virgin. As she saw it, there was no need to feel badly about what she did. Her virginity wasn't a gift -- it couldn't be given or taken. It was more like a line that only she knew was there. And as she had learned with the boy from St. Alban's, no one would even know that line had been crossed unless she told them.

They lay on a blanket in Kevin's living room. He had

turned off the one lamp that had lit the room, and was silhouetted against a yellow light from upstairs where his parents were reliably tucked away. They had grunted their approval at whatever task he had last done for them and were in for the evening. He kissed her. His kisses always tasted like chocolate and tobacco; a mystery for a kid who hardly ever touched either.

Afterward, he wanted to know how she felt. He was backlit from the dim upstairs light, so she searched for where his eyes should be. His voice was earnest. She was fine, she assured him. He relaxed, trailing his finger along the topography of her body.

It had been sweaty and short. She knew better than to think that this was how it was supposed to be. She had had years of doing everything except having sex to know that the act itself should be even better than the build-up. Didn't he know that? Wasn't he the experienced one?

Her virginity meant more to him than it did to her, so she protected him. There was no need for him to know any more than he did. As time wore on, they remained close friends. She tucked away her trump card. After all, he was a really nice boy. She wouldn't need to use it.

They had sex a few more times, but it wasn't much better than the first time. After a few months, she let things fall apart.

He'd be fine, she had reasoned. The cheerleader would be there to pick up the pieces.

4.2

FIRST DATE

I ARRIVED IN THE LOBBY OF THE PARAGON HOTEL.

I had worn jeans and a navy blazer with a ruffled white shirt. I had topped it off with a pair of pink Prada slingbacks. I couldn't help what New Jersey's humidity had done to my hair, so I decided to roll with it.

Damn. I looked so good this morning.

I still looked okay, but I was painfully aware that I was the woman wearing pink pumps and oversized hair at a tech conference.

I took the escalator to the second floor reception area. It deposited me right in the middle of a yawning space with red carpets and a central bank of glass elevators. The hotel rooms encircled an atrium, each with a clear view to reception. I sat at a short bench as far from the elevators as I could manage. A banquette of wood gleamed darkly at me from three sides with a hotel employee stationed every eight feet. The restaurant behind me was packed with conference-goers. I hated these conference hotel behemoths. Besides, it felt as if every person there knew that I didn't belong.

It was impossible to sit at the most flattering angle when I didn't know which direction he'd come from. And what if he spotted me from above?

Shoot. I look fine when I'm standing, but I can't hide this muffin top when I sit.

I adjusted, looked around, and adjusted again. I didn't know which direction he'd be coming from.

Damn. It'll be even worse if he sees me worrying about my belly.

I stopped fidgeting and tried to look nonchalant.

Suddenly, I had an idea. I'd ask for help. I had known Kevin since we dated in high school, and he was a reliable voice of reason. Plus, he seemed to live with his phone by his side, because he usually answered my text messages within minutes. I pulled out my phone and opened a new text message window.

The Dangerous Woman's Guide To Domesticity

> **Hey, what's going on?**
>
> Lily? Is that you?
>
> I thought you were abducted by aliens.
>
> **Nope. Still here.**
>
> Stolen by Bigfoot?
>
> **What the hell are you talking about?**
>
> I'm just trying to figure out what happened to my friend.
>
> Her name is Lilith...

...she's a Capricorn...

...she likes long walks on the beach...

Hey! That's my joke!

So, it IS you!

Whatever.

Seriously, though. I need your help. You're one of my oldest friends.

OK, shoot.

I need you to stop me from doing something stupid. Really stupid.

The Dangerous Woman's Guide To Domesticity

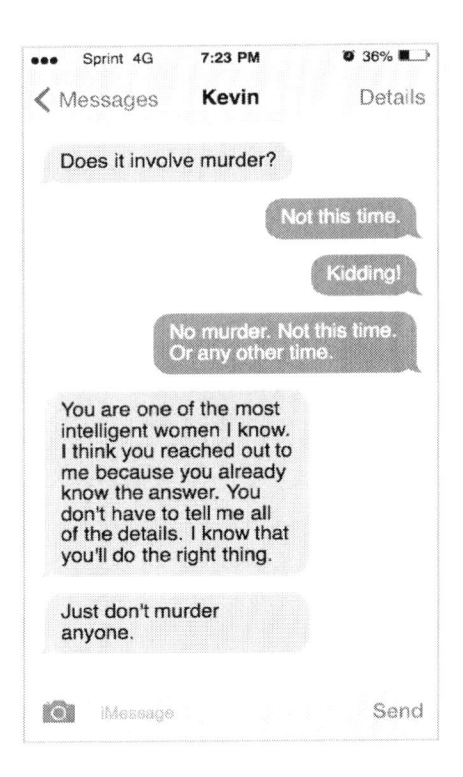

Kevin

Does it involve murder?

Not this time.

Kidding!

No murder. Not this time. Or any other time.

You are one of the most intelligent women I know. I think you reached out to me because you already know the answer. You don't have to tell me all of the details. I know that you'll do the right thing.

Just don't murder anyone.

> **Sprint 4G**   7:26 PM   35%
>
> ‹ Messages   **Kevin**   Details
>
> > Thanks for humoring me. I'm just having a little freakout moment over here.
>
> > I'd better go now. Gotta put a stop to that stupid thing I mentioned earlier.
>
> I'm here 4 U homie.
>
> > ;)
>
> iMessage   Send

Julian seemed to materialize from nowhere, and had clearly seen me first. He was trying to hide a grin. I stood, making slow work of gathering my purse and overnight bag. I willed my heart to stop fluttering. My pulse drummed like a timpani in my ears. There was no way that I was going to put a stop to this. I was all in.

Julian was exactly as I remembered. He was tall with long, muscled limbs that I imagined rippling smoothly under his clothes. He'd always had a bit of an awkward hitch to his gait, but I found it charming, even disarming, when set against the razor-sharp tailoring of his suit. It was his imperfections that made him perfect to me. I took him in. There was the longish nose with the heavy brow atop it; the only feature that gave away how much time had passed. His thick curls had been cropped so close that his hair lay flat against his head.

I don't like that haircut. Thank goodness that there's one thing I don't love about the way he looks.

I felt myself coming unmoored as he approached. That haircut would help me keep one foot on solid ground.

Julian unleashed a full-on smile. God, those lips. Soft, pink and full; they had always made his kisses feel like sex. Sex with him, on the other hand, was far beyond anything I had experienced before or since -- a singular pleasure. I smiled back, unable to do anything else. Here was my cosmic mate; the one person who was made just for me. I felt that old gravitational pull as soon as he appeared, and I was helplessly, deliciously, in his orbit.

We didn't know whether to hug or -- no, of course we wouldn't kiss. Or shake hands -- right? This was soul-crushingly awkward. Mercifully, Julian took my overnight bag. I clutched my purse with two hands. Both our hands were now occupied. That was a relief. I stole a glance at Julian as we rode the elevator to his room in silence.

He's even more nervous than I am. Nervous enough for two people. I think I'll just let him be nervous for both of us.

Once we stepped off of the elevator, he started prattling, almost nonstop. This, too, seemed to indicate his nervousness. It wasn't a conversation, exactly. It was meant to fill the space between then. He went on, in an almost too-formal tone, all the way to his room; while he fumbled with his room key; as we stepped inside.

"I got us a room with two beds so that you would feel more comfortable."

I exhaled with relief. "Thank you," I smiled.

"Well, um, I'll just, um, step outside while you change clothes."

I didn't know whether to feel relief or annoyance at the awkwardness of it all. He was being so wonderful with the double beds; stepping outside so that I could change clothes privately; the adorably stilted conversation.

With Julian waiting in the hallway, I did a quick change. I slid on a pair of high-heeled boots, brushed my hair out and threw on a bright red lipstick. It was a reliable refresh that had me ready to go in three minutes.

* * *

We walked around midtown Manhattan, looking for a place to have dinner. Julian put his hand around my waist as we crossed the street and stayed close to me as we walked. His touch was electric. We wandered for more than an hour, enjoying our chemistry and half-heartedly searching for a quiet place to talk. The night sky clouded over and pedestrian traffic thinned.

We ducked into the nearest restaurant as soon as it began to drizzle.

I placed my order: "May I have the grilled salmon, please? And is it possible to have the green beans without almonds? I have a nut allergy."

"I'll have the pecan-crusted halibut," he said.

Two beds. Pecan-crusted halibut. So, he doesn't expect that we're going to have sex.

I was incredibly attracted to him, but still felt a sense of relief. The pressure to sleep with him was off.

It wasn't exactly his fault that he did so much of the talking at dinner. Our chemistry was palpable; each action from one of us evoking an equal and opposite reaction in the other. He was nervous, so I was not. I was silent, so he talked to fill the void.

I listened to him talk about work. His was a world of money that he had never dreamed of as a kid. He had grown up poor in a section of West Philadelphia that didn't produce many men like him. I understood why making so much money was important to him, but surely there were other things to talk about.

I watched him take a forkful of his dinner. I wouldn't be kissing those lips tonight. Plus, we were going on two hours of discussion about algorithms, office politics and who deserves how many millions of dollars in bonuses. I couldn't relate to those numbers anyway, and couldn't have cared less about someone else's office politics.

Does he even realize that this is going badly?

The adrenaline of seeing him again was wearing off, and I was beginning to tire. I started to zone out.

* * *

Back at the hotel, we began the awkward dance of getting dressed for bed. I had made the mistake of telling him that I normally sleep naked. He stretched across the width of one of the double beds, propped on one elbow.

"So...I guess it's time to get undressed. How are we going to do this?" he grinned. It was less a question than a nudge.

"You must be insane," I replied. "There's no way I'm getting naked right now."

It had been 20 years and three pregnancies since the last

time he'd been in a position to watch me undress. I refused to chicken out and change in the bathroom, so I had to do things carefully. I took off my blouse and slipped on a fine-ribbed stretch cotton nightie, removing my jeans only after it was safely pulled down over my hips. I then slipped my bra straps from my shoulders and unhooked the clasp behind my back, then removed my bra through the scoop neckline of the nightie.

I had undressed like this a hundred times before to hide my naked body from my over-eager husband. Still, my mini-show gave Julian a little something to enjoy. My breasts swelled nicely under the cling of the nightie, which hugged my hips and behind in a way that I knew I could feel good about. I arched my back, stuck out my butt and did a tiny shimmy -- just like I'd practiced in the mirror at home -- before sitting modestly on the other bed.

"Come here." He made room for me and patted the spot beside him.

I was suddenly terrified. *This is what I wanted, right?*

Here was the assertive Julian that I remembered. His nervousness had clearly vanished, making room for my panic. I rose from the bed and sat next to him.

"Closer," he coaxed in a near-whisper.

Wrapping one arm around my waist, Julian pulled me close and adjusted the pillows so that the length of my body lay against his. I could feel his breath on the back of my neck. I tensed at the sudden intimacy.

This is happening. I cannot believe that this is actually happening.

I hadn't been close to anyone besides my husband in 18 years. It felt familiar but somehow foreign. Julian inhaled deeply at the nape of my neck.

He is smelling me. This may be the sexiest thing ever.

He began planting light kisses on my neck and shoulders, and I gave in. I shut off my brain and melted into him.

In one quick move, he flipped me on my back and was on top; his erection pressing into me through his underwear. Propped on his arms, he ground his hips into me and watched my face as a moan escaped my lips. He lowered himself into me for a kiss.

"Wait, *no*!" I scrambled from beneath Julian's weight. He sat upright, alarmed. "You had nuts at dinner. We can't kiss. Not tonight, at least!"

"What the -- oh, shit. I cannot believe this." He sprang from the bed and began pacing.

"Are you sure you're really allergic?"

I gave him a dirty look.

"That was an *hour* ago," he protested.

"It's a problem; trust me," I seethed.

Julian grabbed his phone. "IDIOT! I cannot believe how stupid I am. This is how my life is going right now."

His thumbs jabbed at the screen as he paced.

"Okay," he announced, stopping short. "This study says that the proteins that cause nut allergy are metabolized two hours after eating." He looked up from his screen hopefully.

I shook my head.

He looked back at his screen again for a few moments, thumbs punching furiously.

"And this one says it can take between one and four hours. FUCK!"

I let out a short, bitter laugh. This was absurd.

"If I brush my teeth, can we at least try?" His eyes pleaded.

I looked at him for a long moment, then shrugged. "Sure;

let's give it a try."

It wasn't going to work, but I had to let him do what he could about the situation.

I could hear the sounds of what must have been pretty intensive tooth brushing from the bathroom. Julian had always had oral hygiene that put most people (well, me, really) to shame, but tonight he was seriously motivated. Amusedly, I imagined him using all of his tooth brushing skills to eradicate the offending pecans.

"Don't forget your tongue," I offered.

There was no answer from the bathroom.

Julian finally emerged and strode straight toward me. I opened my mouth to speak and his lips met mine, pressing hard into me while his tongue dipped and swirled inside my mouth. He swept both of my wrists above my head with his left hand and fondled my breast with his right, parting my knees with his and pressing his erection into me. He restrained me with the weight of his body and kissed me until I gasped for air.

"Good?" he asked.

"Very good," I panted.

He dove into me again. He was in command and I was thrilled to let him have everything he wanted. It was what I wanted, too. This was the vigor, the swirling passion I remembered from our college days. I was dizzy with arousal as he got on his knees, sliding me toward him by my hips. He scrambled out of his boxer briefs and paused for a moment.

He was magnificent.

I generally like what the penis can do, not how it looks. Here, too, Julian was exceptional. Forget measurements; it was like we had started as one piece of flesh that had been carved into male and female form. Each time we were put back together was a moment of transcendental ecstasy. And so, form followed perfect function: he was hard and gleaming and completely unrivaled; veined and thickened in places that caused me extraordinary stimulation. His orgasm brought on mine, and mine enhanced his, which in turn heightened mine. Sex with Julian was like a secret of the supernatural.

Again pinning my hands above my head, he kissed me deeply as he tried to slide inside me. I couldn't take him in.

"Oh my god, I'm so nervous," I stammered. "I can't...I--I'm not...."

"It's okay," he said, reassuringly.

"Don't worry, I'll just --" I licked my fingers and smeared my saliva over my labia.

Shit, I am nervous. If I weren't so aroused, I'd be mortified.

I was certainly aroused, but my body had sided with the part of me that was terrified at betraying my marriage. I had pushed those thoughts down deep during my evening with Julian. So deep, apparently, that they went right down to my vagina. I was completely dry. I licked again and inserted two fingers inside me.

"Now try," I whispered.

He slid into me, not as easily as he might have if my body were cooperating. I felt embarrassment rising, then just as quickly decided to ignore the feeling. There was nothing I could do about what had just happened. My bigger concern was the voice screaming in my head.

This is so wrong! You're not this kind of person. This is definitely the dumbest thing you've ever done. Besides, you're not even enjoying it.

Something splashed onto my left eyelid. I reflexively

squeezed my eye shut and turned away. He was sweating. A lot. And no wonder: He was humping as fast and furiously as a teenager who has finally gotten the chance to do it with a real, live other person. He wiped his brow and kept humping.

This was not at all what I remembered. This sweaty humping was not doing our history any justice. I'd have to take the situation into my own hands. We switched positions, with me on top. I settled onto him slowly, working him in while watching his face.

He had always been silent when we made love, which I had previously taken as a bit of a personal challenge. This time, I didn't worry about him making any sound. His face said it all. With our eyes locked, his lips froze into a gorgeous pink O. He was completely inside me now.

I sat directly atop his hips and held his gaze. I leaned back a bit, resting my right hand on his thigh. My left hand on his belly, I did a little serpentine thing with my hips to settle him into the right spot. Slow, deliberate, searching. Stop. There it was. The magic spot.

I worked him from that spot, undulating slowly so that I could feel all of him. I locked his hips in place with my knees, squeezing him tightly. He understood, daring not to change anything with his own strokes. I saw his eyes wash over my body, and he shuddered a bit.

It felt amazing. It was everything that I remembered about us. I closed my eyes and gave in to a feeling that I had missed for so long. My hips started to move as if on their own. I felt warm all over as an instinctual, almost animal feeling took over. And I loved that he was watching me.

I opened my eyes. Something had changed. He was still

watching me, but his face was different. I slowed to a rhythmic grind, watching.

"Did you climax already?" I tried not to sound disappointed. I already knew the answer.

He nodded.

He wasn't exactly a smooth talker. He was genuinely thunderstruck, and his sweet nothings were really just questions. He was sweetly hyperbolic, though; his exaggerations emphasizing the point.

"You know how you hear about women in history who wars get started over? You are that type of woman. Every single man was looking at you when we were out tonight."

"Whoa, I think you need to take it down a notch," I teased.

"Okay; you're right. Not *every* single man was looking at you." He paused, suddenly serious again.

"There's something about you. I mean, there are beautiful women everywhere, but there's something about you. Are you like this with other people? Am I the only one who reacts to you this way? Is it like this with your husband?"

I demurred: "There's no right way to answer that question."

He went on, ignoring my protest: "You know, when we were in college, I used to agonize about the day when you would realize that you could do so much better than dating me." His voice dropped to a whisper. "We missed so much time together. You truly are the love that I miss every day."

This was amazing. He was holding me close with our foreheads pressed together. Our noses nearly touching, we inhaled our commingled breath. This was something that we had never really done when we were kids. He had always pushed away from this type of intimacy. I never would have imagined that I was his personal Helen of Troy. These were words that I would have killed to have heard when we were together.

"You completely own me," he said. "I would do anything you asked me to do. Anything."

He wanted me to ask him to do something. Something big.

My cheeks suddenly hot, I searched for a distraction. My fingers sought the nape of his neck. I let them idle there for a moment, then trailed them up the back of his head. His curls used to coil silkily around my fingers, and now they were gone. I felt his breath catch.

Focus on the haircut. That vanilla haircut.

I closed my eyes and imagined fat coils of Julian's hair being swept into a dustpan and dumped into a trash bin.

His body relaxed, and the tension broke.

5.1

THREE GREAT LOVES

THE AUGUST AIR WAS HEAVY AND MOIST. THE DAY'S heat had been unrelenting, and had lasted well into the evening. Lily's two-room apartment was reasonably cool. Its window-unit air conditioner cooled its small space easily. But still, she felt restless. She wasn't sure what she was looking for, but she could almost always count on rely on her neighborhood for entertainment. She lived in one of the most lively neighborhoods in Chicago, full of young singles and late-night storefronts to welcome their endless activity.

She strolled past gay couples holding hands as they walk down the street, listening to whatever snippets of their conversations that she could catch. Walking down the street was kind of like channel surfing; a way to sample scenes from other people's lives. There were elderly people walking their tiny dogs. The dogs pulled impudently on their retractable leashes, little legs blurring as they crossed from one side of the sidewalk to the other. Runners zipped past, their breath huffing along with their footfalls.

Lily was grateful that the runners stirred the still air just a little.

She walked past the burrito place on the corner with the giant plate glass windows. There was a line snaking all the way to the door. A young couple squeezed just inside the doors, trying to get in line without waiting outside. She checked her watch. It was after 8:00 and she hadn't eaten anything since lunch. She considered a burrito, but it was too hot to eat right now. Thinking about dinner reminded her that she needed to buy groceries. Lily took a quick mental inventory of her refrigerator. She was pretty sure that she had salad dressing, mustard, two eggs, an onion and some salad greens that were starting to go bad. She couldn't put it off any longer. She would need to pick up some food tonight. She strolled in the general direction of the grocery store.

She stopped in front of the tattoo parlor and examined the sample designs in the window. She had played with the idea of getting a tattoo for a long time, but couldn't decide on a design that she would want to keep forever. She looked inside as she walked past the open door, and could see a young woman lying on her stomach, having an elaborate design inked on her back. Lily was fascinated by people who could make such a permanent choice. She had only ever gone wild with things that she could remove from her body, like clothes or accessories. Even her nail polish was perpetually conservative. Her manicure colors ranged from sheer off-white to sheer baby pink. Still, she looked everywhere for inspiration. One day, she reasoned, she would find something that would inspire her to permanently ink it into her skin.

Lily kept strolling, and passed a narrow storefront with a small awning. The words "Palm Reader" covered the glass at eye level, with a vintage palmistry graphic underneath. She slowed, taking a closer look at the annotations on the giant palm. Suddenly self-conscious, she ducked into the sex shop next door. She didn't think of herself as someone who believed in things like palm reading, but she was curious. What if there was some truth to it? Lily absent-mindedly pretended to browse the dildos while considering whether to go into the palm reader's shop.

She heard tittering behind her. Two friends huddled together, one holding a gigantic, realistic-looking dark brown dildo.

"Oh my god," gushed the first woman. She gazed at the dildo, stroking it. "I've never had a black boyfriend before."

"Definitely get that one. Everyone needs a big black cock," her friend replied.

Lily sighed. She couldn't let the situation go unanswered. "Ladies," she purred, sidling closer to them. "Let me assure you, that --" she nodded toward the giant dildo "-- only exists on a few freaks. Thank goodness that most men are quite ordinary. Even black men."

The two women looked mortified. That was fine with Lily. She didn't like being reduced to a body part, and didn't want that to happen to anyone else, either. If those ladies were shopping for monster dildos, they were in the right place. But if they were looking for a black boyfriend, they could go out and get one.

It occurred to her that she was lecturing strangers in a sex shop in order to avoid going to the palm reader. It was time to leave.

She walked back to the shop next door. The palm reader rose from behind a glass cabinet. She was chewing, and wiped her hands on a napkin before walking across the room to greet Lily. "Oh, good. You're here," she said, gesturing to a seat at a small table. "Forgive me; I was just finishing dinner. I'll just wash my hands." She disappeared behind a curtain, and Lily heard the sound of water running.

The palm reader emerged a few moments later. Lily was struck by how ordinary she looked. She wore jeans and a beautiful silk blouse printed with a tonal indigo gingko leaf pattern. She had long hair and a soft voice. This was very different from everything Lily had ever seen on TV about palmistry. She started to relax. Even if the reading turned out to be a load of junk, Lily was cynically comforted by the fact that she'd be helping to fund the palm reader's beautiful blouse collection.

Beyond her concern that it was a waste of money, Lily secretly worried that the palm reader would give her terrible news. She gave the reader her hands, looking at them as intently as the woman across the table. She had no idea what her hands were telling the reader, but didn't want to telegraph her nervousness. The palm reader swept her thumb over Lily's palm and took a closer look, leaning in and lifting Lily's hand closer to her face. She looked surprised. Lily resisted the urge to ask what she saw.

"You're going to have a long life and good health."

"Really? That's great!" Lily tried her best not to snatch her hands away. If the palm reader looked at her hands much longer, she might see something devastating.

"There is one more thing," said the reader, turning Lily's hand slightly to get a better look. "You're going to have three great loves in your life."

Lily laughed out loud, relieved. This had not gone the way she had expected. She thought that the whole point of the experience was for the palm reader to share a grim prediction in order to hook her customers. Instead, "three great loves" was the hook. She paid the palm reader and headed toward the grocery store.

Three great loves. It was an intriguing proposition. She could immediately think of two. There was Kevin, her high school boyfriend, and Julian, her on-again, off-again college love. And the third? Who might that be? Lily imagined the palm reader's calculation that she would be a reliable repeat customer, curious to know if every new man she met would be one of her three.

She was still thinking about the three great loves of her life as she walked home, struggling with two heavy armloads of groceries. Julian was definitely one. He was quite possibly her first great love. Was Kevin really another? Maybe, maybe not. And who would the third person be?

Suddenly, the bottom of one of the grocery bags split. Groceries spilled out of the bottom of the bag, and cans rolled in opposite directions onto the grass. Lily cursed herself for buying cans of tuna without a grocery cart to wheel the whole load home.

Two pint-sized dogs on retractable leashes nosed at her groceries. "Oh, what happened, Moopsie?" the elderly owner's voice simpered. "Did someone drop their groceries? Oh, what did you find? Is it broccoli?" The old woman stood and let her dogs rummage through the food as Lily struggled to collect the fallen items. She bristled at the thought of a dog nosing her produce, but decided to keep her mouth shut to avoid being disrespectful to the old woman.

She heard the familiar footfall and simultaneous huff of a runner, who slowed to a stop behind her. She stood and was startled to find herself face-to-face with a handsome man with a dazzling smile. He handed her two containers of yogurt. "I'll help you with these," he said, still breathing heavily. "Ma'am, would you mind moving your dogs?" The old woman shot him a dirty look before moving along, dogs leading the way. He picked up a few more items and redistributed them in the remaining bags.

"By the way, I'm Aaron," he said.

"Aaron," she repeated, committing the movement of her lips and tongue to memory as she said his name. "I'm Lily."

Aaron scooped the bags in both hands. "I'll help you get these home."

"I'd like that," Lily smiled. "Thank you."

5.2

EVOLUTION

THE VALET WAVED ME FORWARD. I INCHED my car closer to the rear bumper of the car ahead until he directed me to stop.

I reached down to the floor of the passenger seat. I had taken a turn hard and fast about a block ago, and my purse had spilled its contents onto the floor. The valet walked to my side of the car and opened the door.

"Welcome to the Obsidian Hotel and Spa, Miss. Will you be staying with us today?"

"Yes, thank you. I'm under 'Armstrong'."

Under Armstrong, on top of Armstrong, Armstrong with my legs behind my head....

I couldn't resist the double entendre. I fished on the floor for my pen and a pack of gum to hide my grin from the valet. He wrote something on a card in his hand, tore off the bottom third of the card and stuck it under my windshield wiper.

"Enjoy your stay, Mrs. Armstrong."

Its contents tucked safely inside, I grabbed my purse and swiveled my legs around to exit the car. I imagined how it must have looked: My skirt riding up my legs as my stiletto-clad feet touched to the ground. I watched the valet take a not-so-discreet look at my thighs. I stood. My sexuality felt big. It seemed to push outward like an aura around me.

"Oh, I'm not Mrs. Armstrong," I smiled, cocking my head.

I pretended not to notice that I had moved a little too close. I let my arm brush against his mid-section as I walked past.

He smiled a little. "Are the keys in the car?" His voice quavered a bit.

"They're in the ignition," I replied, holding his gaze.

To my own surprise, I didn't feel badly about what I was doing. I didn't care about the valet. I couldn't possibly be the first person he's seen who's having an affair. How would the hotel workers even know that I was there with someone who's not my husband? Even if they did figure it out, what would they do about it? They didn't want to risk losing our business. I had learned to enjoy the heady high that came with flouting the rules.

It was about more than just rebelliousness. I had held my nose or looked the other way when it came to so many of my own clients' transgressions, smiling and pretending that I didn't hate what they were doing. In a perverse way, it felt good to make someone else uncomfortable for a change.

This was our fifth meeting since our reunion in New York. Before then, our text messages and phone calls were mostly teasing and trepidation. Each of us was a more than a little nervous about how an actual meeting would go. Would we still like each other? Would we still be attracted to each other? Would he be able to perform? Would I? Or would we be two pathetic exes trying to revive something that was stone dead? Would the sex be as good as it once was?

After New York, our conversations took a hard turn. Everything was about how and when we could get together again. He offered to fly me to wherever he was -- a conference, a big meeting or any location that we could get to easily.

This time, we were in Houston. I went to the front desk as instructed and picked up the key that Julian had left for me there. He would meet me in the room at the end of his afternoon conference session.

I took off my shoes and washed my hands. The flight had been bumpy, and I needed a little time to relax. I changed my top, washed my face and reapplied my makeup. Then I laid face-up on the bed and stared at the ceiling, enjoying the silence.

After a few minutes, I rolled onto my stomach and grabbed my phone. I wanted to find a place to eat tonight. It was very easy for us to lose track of time on our trysts. The last couple of times that we spent the night together, we wrapped up our lovemaking too late to get decent food. We had ordered bad pizza twice in a row because we had missed room service. I didn't want to do that again.

There was a window at the far side of the room. I got up to check out the view. There wasn't much to see from here. This wasn't like the Las Vegas or Denver hotels where we had stayed, where the views were part of the entertainment. This room overlooked a concrete parking garage. There wasn't much to see beyond it, either. We were only on the ninth floor.

I saw an unusual movement. A couple had exited the staircase onto the roof, where there were no other cars parked.

They kissed, slowly at first, then escalated to making out more intensely. I felt a little thrill, watching them. I was standing at the window and could see them clearly, but they couldn't see me at all. I wondered if the hotel's windows were mirrored or tinted. It would be embarrassing to get caught watching them. Even more embarrassing than getting caught in the act myself.

The door unlocked with an electronic whir and a click of the deadbolt. I turned to look. Julian had just walked in with two bottles of my favorite sparkling water and a cup full of lime wedges. I grinned and gestured for him to join me at the window, then pointed to the couple making out. Julian watched for a moment.

"You like that?" he asked, gesturing toward the couple.

"You should have seen it. They snuck away like the garage roof was the only place they could find. Now look at them." I was transfixed.

Julian positioned himself behind me and kissed my neck. I stuck my behind out, rubbing it back and forth against him.

Julian stepped backward, arms outstretched. "Now look at what you just did!"

"Did I do that?"

I turned away from the window, leaned against the window frame and fixed my gaze on his erection. It strained against his pants. It was beautiful.

"Yes, you did," he replied in a mock-accusatory tone. "And I want to know what you're going to do about it."

I moved toward him slowly, letting my eyes trail from the bulge in his pants to his face.

"I'm so, so sorry. I didn't mean to do that."

I held his gaze as I knelt in front of him. The bulge

twitched. I unbuckled his belt and unhooked his pants, still looking into his eyes.

"Please let me help you with that." I kissed the bulge and unzipped his pants. "Please. Will you let me, baby?"

His erection found my mouth like a heat-seeking missile. I kissed it again, and let my lips tickle it through his underwear.

"Let me suck it, baby." Julian collapsed against the wall.

* * *

I rolled onto my stomach and looked at my phone screen. It was 8:14. "Oh my god. It's been three hours!" I shook my head in disbelief at Julian. A broad grin spread across his face as he looked at me. I grinned, too. He was so damned gorgeous.

"I'm starving," Julian said, still grinning.

"Me, too." My stomach rumbled loudly, as if on cue. "Hey, do you like noodles? I heard about a place that serves nothing but noodles and whiskey."

Julian looked doubtful. "Is this a real place?"

"Oh, yeah. It's real." I raked my fingers through my hair and gave him a wink. "Just stick with me, kid."

"I plan to," he replied.

We dressed and made our way out into the night air.

I had found a secret restaurant -- one of those places that looks like nothing from the outside and that requires a password to get in. It featured more than 150 whiskeys from across the U.S. and from what I had heard, their noodle dishes were pretty killer. Besides its understated cool, it seemed like the kind of place where we could have a bite to eat without being spotted.

"Deja vu," I spoke into the open slot in the door.

I had looked up tonight's password on my phone, and double-checked it before knocking. Julian and I exchanged a look. This experience had promised to be awesome -- if we could actually get in. The slot slid shut and the door opened outward. The air inside was cool and wafted with an unidentifiable savory note.

"Welcome, folks," said a burly man with tattoo sleeves.

He was bobbing lightly to a throbbing rhythmic hip-hop beat playing in the background. He swiveled on his stool and picked up two tasting glasses of whiskey, offering them to us with a nod.

"A little taste to kick things off tonight. This is a toasted barrel rye. We just got this one in, and personally, I love it."

"I like this place already," Julian remarked, lifting his glass to me.

I lifted my glass in return and sipped my taste of whiskey. It had a silky texture and a distinctive vanilla note. I enthusiastically nodded my approval to the tattooed man while rolling the liquid on my tongue.

"If you like that, you should try the Copper Trail flight," the tattooed man added.

"Appreciate it, man." Julian handed our glasses back to him.

"No problem," he replied. "Enjoy yourselves."

We followed the hostess into the dim dining area, which was really more a series of nooks. One group of seats was clustered around a fireplace. Another, an elevated section in the center of the room, was roped off with stanchions and red velvet rope. A DJ was set up with a laptop and headphones, churning out a steady flow of laid-back hip-hop beats with a few old-school favorites thrown in. The ceiling was low and and finished with what looked like reclaimed wood. The center area made the tallest diners duck to their seats. No one actually hit their heads, but the low clearance made them cautious.

Julian and I were guided to a nook with three booths, each made to look even more intimate with a single dim vintage bulb suspended from the ceiling. He ushered me to one side of the booth, then moved to sit on the other side.

"Wait," I scooted over a tiny bit on the banquette and gave him an inviting look. "Sit here, with me."

He smiled a little and accepted, sitting so close that our shoulders touched.

When our server arrived, we ordered the Copper Trail flight. We picked up our menus and reviewed the house specialties.

"This one looks good," Julian pointed to a beef bowl with broth before pointing to a pork-based bowl. "This does, too."

I plucked the menu out of his hands and tossed it to the other side of the table. I leaned into him and pointed to an appetizer, positioning my menu so that he's have to come closer to see.

"Ooh, that does look good. What else should we order?"

I watched Julian's face change as he picked up on my cue. He slid closer to me, almost imperceptibly, while we chose an edamame starter and a side of pan-seared mixed greens.

* * *

Our drinks flight had arrived and we had just placed our

order. Julian seemed to have moved even closer, with his arm tossed on the back of the banquette and the fingers of one hand grazing my shoulder. We shared the sampling of whiskey, sipping from the same glass and murmuring our reviews of this oak-y one or that spice-laden one while Julian trailed the finger of his other hand up and down my thigh.

"So," I said, holding his gaze. "It seems that your fingers are walking the copper trail." I gave him a suggestive look. "I hear there's something very interesting at the end of it."

Julian responded by walking his fingers up my thigh until they made their way under my skirt. I sighed lightly at the unexpected tickle.

He paused. "Are you wearing underwear?"

"I think you know the answer to that." I still held his gaze.

"But, you're wearing a skirt," he blurted.

"I am."

He put his head in his hands, elbows on the table.

"What's wrong?" I smirked. I rubbed his lower back in small circles. "You look upset."

He looked around. "Where's the bathroom?"

"I don't know," I replied. "I think it's over there...it's probably somewhere near the kitchen."

"Don't you have to use the bathroom?" He looked at me sidewise.

"No, I don't." I gave him the most innocent look I could muster.

He stood, suddenly. His glass skidded shortly on the table. He caught it before it reached the edge, placed it in the center of the table and walked away without a word.

I closed my eyes. My pulse thrummed in my ears. Wait

sixty heartbeats. Not quite a minute. Then walk.

I counted in silence, then stood and walked to the bathrooms. They were two unisex, single-stall private rooms. I knocked on the first door.

"Are you okay?" No answer.

After a moment, I tried the second door.

"Julian? Are you okay?"

The door opened and Julian pulled me inside by the wrist. I couldn't help a smile as he pulled me to him, our chests bumping lightly.

I fumbled with his belt buckle. Julian swept my hands aside, releasing his pants in what seemed like a single move. They fell down to his knees. I reached inside his underwear and wrapped him in my hand. We kissed. I ran the tip of my tongue just inside of his upper lip, then gently sucked his lower lip into my mouth, biting it lightly. His erection grew hotter and harder in my hand.

We shuffled to the toilet, kissing and trying not to trip over his pants. Julian sat on the toilet. I straddled him, lifting my skirt to my hips. His erection stood straight up, waiting for me. He laced his fingers through mine and I lowered myself onto him.

He grabbed my ass and pulled me close, then buried himself into me. He felt incredible. I couldn't help my own movement. I arched back, placed my hands on his knees, and moved my hips, keeping him deep inside me.

Someone knocked on the door and tried the handle. I returned to reality for just a second.

I'm pretty sure that I locked the door behind us. Kind of sure, at least. Actually, I don't remember.

I couldn't remember with certainty whether I'd locked the

door, but I couldn't find it in myself to worry about it. Nothing mattered in that moment but Julian and me. I was intoxicated by him.

I planted my feet on the floor and stood, nearly pulling off of him. He looked shocked. I relaxed and pushed him into me, then squeezed as I lifted my hips, stroking the head of his penis as deftly as if I were using my hand. His hands went to my hips to pull me onto him again. I pulled back until just the very tip of him was inside me.

"Oh, no, baby," I whispered in his ear, "I want you to ask nicely."

I let my breath tickle his ear. He removed his hands. I rewarded him by stroking the head again. I was sure that it felt good. I hadn't done all those Kegels for nothing.

Ohmygod, he mouthed.

I lowered my hips, taking in about three-quarters of his length for just one stroke before working the tip again.

"What was that?" I breathed into his ear. "Did you say something?"

His lead lolled. His hands went back to my hips.

"Oh, should I stop?" I teased.

His body convulsed and he spat out a short laugh as he moved his hands. "Don't -- *please* don't -- I need..."

I pulled off again until only the very tip was inside me. "What do you need, baby?"

"I need to fuck you. Please. I need to fuck you so bad."

I slammed onto him. As much as I loved teasing him, I really needed him, too.

He held my hips and hammered into me. I felt him expand suddenly, throbbing so strongly that it set off an orgasm. I felt a hot wetness inside me. We sat together for a few seconds, spent. I kissed him deeply, then pulled off. He offered me a handful of toilet paper. I wiped the trail of wetness that had run down my leg. We adjusted our clothes, grinning stupidly at each other.

There were two steaming bowls of noodles, struck through with pork belly, waiting for us when we got back to our table. We dove in.

Julian stopped short. "These are the best noodles that I have had in my entire life," he said solemnly.

I stopped, too. "That," I said, grinning, "is exactly what I was just going to say."

* * *

We left the restaurant full and happy. The night air felt as balmy and humid as a tepid bath.

"It feels so delicious out here." I let the words languish. I felt amazing. "Let's not go back yet. Let's grab some coffee or something."

"If that's what you want, let's do it." Julian looked as content as I felt.

We found a small pastry shop that was open late. The patio was tiny and idyllic, with a candy-colored awning and intricate wrought-iron chairs and tables. We sat and sipped iced coffee at one of the smaller tables.

"It's a good thing we don't have children." Julian started.

"Why?"

I felt a bit hurt. I had once dreamed of marrying him and having children together. That seemed like a long time ago.

"Well, our children would probably starve."

I gave him a look, not sure where he was going with this.

"They'd probably go around, begging the neighbors for food. I can hear them now: 'Yeah, our parents are in there, but they're...you know...making more babies.'"

I swallowed a mouthful of iced coffee and exploded into a full-throated laugh.

"Oh my god, you're right." I wiped tears from the corners of my eyes. "We would be the worst parents. We'd just spend all of our time screwing."

I paused, still smiling.

"I guess it's a good thing that we didn't end up together."

Julian watched me come down from my laugh.

"Well, we wouldn't be able to get married for at least another six years. That's when Alex leaves for college."

He had said it so softly that I knew he wasn't joking.

I was silent. I put my lips to my drink to keep my jaw from dropping.

"And our kids wouldn't really starve. You're an excellent mother."

I nearly choked on my coffee. At one point, I had genuinely wanted to spend the rest of my life with Julian. The failure of our early relationship was devastating to me. I had spent years telling myself that I had had it wrong; that he wasn't right for me and that I was a stupid, desperate girl for wanting to be with him. I had to shut this conversation down. It was too painful.

I blurted the first thing that came to mind: "Forty-seven! I can't be pregnant at 47. I can't be pregnant again at all. I'm done."

"I understand." Julian spoke quietly. "But, you know, maybe you'll feel differently. Maybe as this relationship evolves..."

"This," I sputtered, gesturing back and forth between the two of us, "is not evolving into anything."

I wanted to jump onto the table and scream at him.

This relationship can't turn into anything more than it is now! We're both married! We made our choices a long time ago! This is an affair! There are rules!

"You don't know that," he said. He sounded wounded. "You don't know that. You can't see the future."

I decided not to argue. I hadn't seen him this vulnerable before. In fact, I would have killed for him to have been this open with me when we were together.

"You're right. I don't know what will happen in the future." I conceded the point.

We sat in silence. He watched me sip my coffee.

"I want to show you something," he said.

His tone made me leery. "What is it?" I asked, suddenly cautious.

He unbuttoned three buttons at the top of his shirt and exposed a tattoo of a labyrinthine maze. It was round, nearly four inches in diameter, and beautifully crafted in bold black ink. I had noticed it before, of course, and I had asked when he had it done and whether it had hurt. I had specifically avoided asking about its meaning. There were some stories that I had chosen to sidestep. I accepted that his life had been interesting enough without me, but I didn't want to be reminded of that fact any more than was necessary.

Julian's fingers lingered over the tattoo for a moment. He watched me as I looked at it from across the table.

"This isn't just any maze," he started. "It's a labyrinth.

There's only one way in or out. And the entrance..." he looked down at his chest and pointed to the single opening in the design before looking back at me, "...the entrance to the labyrinth, which is also the only way out, is right at my heart."

I nodded.

"Do you remember when I told you how I met my wife?"

"I do."

This sure as hell had better not be a story about her. I tried to suppress the hot feeling of annoyance rising in my belly.

"I got this shortly after I started dating--."

"Why are you telling me this?"

"Just let me finish."

"OK." I sank back into my seat. I was pissed. "Go on. I won't interrupt."

He took a deep breath. "It was right after the last time you and I had seen each other. I was hoping that you would take me back, but you didn't. That was the moment when I realized that you were completely over me."

"That's not fair," I started.

"You said you wouldn't interrupt." His voice was gentle.

I threw up my hands in a gesture of surrender.

"So, you were done with me. I felt like shit for weeks."

My heart lurched. Our last breakup was complicated. He was wrong; I had never gotten over him.

"Anyway, you remember my best friend from back then, right?" he leaned forward as if to re-engage me.

"Yes. Your friend Paul."

"Right. Well, Paul knew what had happened between us. He gave me this beautiful leather-bound journal with this labyrinth embossed on the front."

He pulled his shirt back, exposing the tattoo once more, then buttoned his shirt as he continued.

"So I wrote. I filled that journal. Used every page. For the first time, I put down all of the feelings I had when I was with you. I had never felt anything as intensely before."

I shifted uncomfortably.

"And then I met Jessica. Paul actually introduced us."

I looked away. I didn't like where this was going, and I was certain that I wasn't ready to hear what he had to say next.

"But even after I met her; even when things got to the point where I thought that relationship would take off, I knew that my whole life would be about making my way back to you."

I lost all feeling in my legs. I silently gave thanks that I was sitting down.

"So, the labyrinth, which begins and ends at my heart, is a reminder that no matter where I go, I am lost until I'm back with you."

"I... I don't know what to...."

My cheeks burned as I stammered. I couldn't even put words together.

"You don't have to say anything."

We finished our drinks and walked back to the hotel.

"Good evening, Mr. Armstrong," said the valet. It was the same man who had parked my car earlier in the day. He opened the glass entry door for us and gave me a nod. "Mrs. Armstrong."

*　*　*

My flight was at 6:20. That meant I would have to leave by

4:00 to get there with a little more than an hour before takeoff. And in order to leave by 4:00, I estimated, I would have to say goodbye to Julian by 2:00. I had learned the hard way that time did funny things when we were together.

Saying goodbye always made me melt into a puddle. I didn't want to leave. He kissed me like I belonged to him, and while we were together, it was easy to believe that I actually did.

I had pretended to check the room for any small items I might have left behind. He had pretended to help me. And now, I was standing before him with my bags in my hand. It was 2:06. Time to say goodbye.

I felt a bit shy. This was always really hard. I decided to go first.

"Well, it was really good to see you again."

He laughed and shook his head, then cleared his throat.

"Yes. It was very good to see you again, too." His voice softened. "It's always so good to see you."

"Well, I guess I should..."

Julian closed the space between us before I could finish and locked his lips with mine. He slipped my purse off of my shoulder and kissed me deeply as it fell to the floor. I could hear my keys jangle at the impact. They sounded like they were far, far away.

Julian picked me up and put me on the dresser. I reached out to grab the TV, which had wobbled threateningly when I bumped against it. Julian pulled me to him by my hips, the bulge in his pants finding my most sensitive spot right through my jeans.

One of his hands found its way up my blouse and squeezed my left breast. His kiss alone made me so crazy that I hardly noticed that the other hand had somehow unbuttoned and unzipped my jeans. He was everywhere. It was like Julian had four hands.

He had started unbuttoning my blouse, kissing the swell of my cleavage. Now that my mouth was free, I tried to protest.

"I have to... I have to... get going...."

Everything he did felt so good that even I didn't believe my own words. I was glad that I had budgeted two hours to get out of there.

I slipped my hips off of the dresser and stood. The head rush made me fall into him, and we nearly fell, together, onto the bed. I laughed and looked away, embarrassed at how crazy I was with arousal. He bit my exposed neck. I felt a surge of heat between my legs. Julian steadied me and knelt between my feet. He slipped his hands down the back of my pants and along my bottom, pushing my jeans down past my hips. He licked along the length of my lips and I convulsed.

I made the 6:20 flight, but just barely. The gate attendants saw me running down the terminal, waving for them to hold the door.

"Thank you so much. My girls would be so disappointed if I missed this flight home." I was nearly out of breath.

"Don't worry about it," the gate agent said. She gave me a kind smile and winked. "Enjoy your flight."

I grinned back at her.

* * *

The newscast droned away on my phone. I had taken it into the shower with me, which I was pretty sure was bad for my phone, but I enjoyed my morning news.

I leaned in close to the mirror, inspecting my face. I dabbed a bit of concealer under my eyes, which instantly brightened my face. I had always been pretty sparing with makeup, preferring to stay away from the type of artistically-applied and perfectly-shaded eyeshadow and contouring that pouting, pretty YouTube girls made seem so easy to do.

I had wasted thousands of dollars on new colors and formulations over the last 25 years, only to return to a version of the same makeup I wore as a teenager: light powder foundation, mascara and lip gloss. A hint of color on my cheeks.

The only new addition to my repertoire was my concealer. It was after Inanna was born that I went to a Bloomingdale's makeup counter. Somehow, I just didn't seem like myself. I was breastfeeding and sleep-deprived. The disembodied smooshiness of postpartum had left me feeling like I was swimming in an ocean of myself. I could accept all of that, because I was convinced that it would all pass. I had done it twice before: The baby would grow up and sleep through the night. She would be weaned. I would work out until my body returned to one that I recognized. But looking in the mirror, I saw what I could only describe as a shadow of myself. It would take time for my body to recover, but I could transform my face with makeup right away. I took myself to Nordstrom the very next day.

"Aaaaand let's just add a bit of concealer under your eyes to get rid of those dark circles."

The makeup artist had dabbed the concealer under my left eye before I had a chance to object. I could feel her breath on my face as she dabbed the sponge against my skin. She swept a mirror into my hand and guided it so that it was level with my face.

"Wait, what? I don't have dark circles...." I shifted my look from her to the mirror.

There was the proof, staring back at me in the mirror. The right side of my face was bright and refreshed. That was me. The un-concealed side of my face looked sunken and shadowed. The makeup artist coughed lightly and tapped her makeup brush on the counter, then shook it lightly. If she were a gunslinger, this would be the moment when she'd blow the smoke from the barrel of the gun she just fired.

"Oh," I conceded. "Those dark circles."

She nodded and dabbed some under my other eye. And so, concealer was added to my makeup routine.

The difference was magical. Even though it had been six years since I'd sat in that concealer-slinging makeup artist's chair, I still marveled at the difference. Like today. I had just gotten out of the shower. The steam had plumped my skin nicely and gave my cheeks a dewy-pink glow. I leaned in close, examining my face in the mirror. This was the look I wished I could keep all day. Then again, if I could manage to keep that dewy, plump, fresh-from-the-shower look, I'd bottle and sell it with the same self-assured cool of the concealer lady. I dabbed the concealer under my eyes.

There I was. It was me, or, at least, the me that I wanted to be. The irony was glaring: To get to the version of myself I liked most, I had to conceal something.

I shook my head at my reflection in the mirror. "So, now we're drawing life lessons from our makeup?" I narrowed my eyes at myself and immediately took note of the little lines that didn't entirely go away when I relaxed my eyes again.

I sighed and reached for the foundation.

I heard feet padding on the bedroom carpet, and Morgan poked her head into the bathroom.

"Mom, I don't have any more toothpaste." She held up a mostly-empty tube of toothpaste. Her fingers weren't quite strong enough to get the last of the toothpaste out of the tube.

I grabbed my newly-opened toothpaste out of my vanity drawer. "Here, take mine."

"Thanks, mom," she chirped as she turned on her heel and padded out through my bedroom.

"You're welcome, sweetie."

"Wait, what's the weather going to be like today?" Morgan reappeared and grabbed my phone, unlocked it and opened the weather app. I made a mental note to change my password again.

Morgan had walked off with my phone. I kept my ears open for the newscaster's transition to a new story. There had been another school shooting two days before, and I wanted to keep Morgan and Inanna away from that kind of news until I had a chance to explain it to them.

I'd give Morgan a minute or two with my phone. For the moment, I was rendered immobile by my mascara application. I once knew a woman with jet black hair and bright blue eyes, who was a dead ringer for Linda Carter, the Wonder Woman of my girlhood. This woman had the longest eyelashes I had ever seen. I had seen her apply makeup at work a couple of times, chatting away and chewing gum while jabbing the spiky mascara wand at her lash line. Her application skills were truly impressive. She could even apply mascara while driving. My applications skills were decidedly inferior to hers.

I leaned over the counter to get as close to the bathroom

mirror as I could, then willed myself not to blink as I swept the applicator along my lashes. My mouth hung open. It was a necessary part of my makeup routine. I had learned through experience that as long as I keep my mouth open, I won't blink. Forget about driving; I can't even talk when I'm putting my mascara on.

"Morgan!" I called, mascara finally done. "I need my phone back."

Inanna walked into the bathroom in her underwear, staring at the phone screen, swiping furiously. She had a pair of jeans slung over her shoulder. My heart leapt. Julian had sent me a series of pictures late last night that were not safe for anyone to see. Just as quickly as the thought occurred to me, I remembered that I had deleted them.

"Thank you, baby doll." I held out my hand for the phone. Inanna reluctantly handed it over.

I took a look at my screen. "The high temperature is going to be...105 degrees?"

"Noooooo," replied Inanna, plucking the phone from my hands again.

In the few moments they had my phone, the girls had added New York, Paris, Phoenix, Denver, London, San Francisco and Dubai to my list of tracked cities. I was looking at Dubai's high temperature. Inanna had quieted down. I realized that she was quietly adding more cities to the list.

"I'll take that," I said, taking the phone back and putting it on the countertop.

"Mom, can you help me put my jeans on?" Inanna looked up at me with her extra-large brown eyes ringed with a dark fringe of long lashes that I had just tried to create with mascara.

"What? Why?" We had been through this before, and I wasn't going to let her get away with feigning helplessness.

I dabbed a bit of too-red lip gloss on my fingertip and applied it to my cheeks. Rather than throw the offending lip gloss away, I had managed to repurpose it. It turned out that this was the best blush color I'd ever used.

"I need help," Inanna insisted.

I turned to her. "You just managed to set my phone to track the weather Sao Paulo. I don't think you need help. Put your pants on, kid."

Inanna looked uncertain.

"Do you want to put them on right here?" I offered.

"Yeah!" her eyes brightened. She sat right down on the floor, and put her feet into her pants.

"I want to listen to that!" Kali called from her bedroom.

"Turn on the wireless speaker," I called back to her. I restarted the story so that she could hear it from the beginning.

Morgan "Oh, is that about that really old woman? She's like, 120 years old! Yeah, I want to hear that story, too!"

Kali walked in without knocking. "The speaker isn't working." She turned the cube over in her hands and shrugged at me.

I thought through the possibilities. "Is your phone still paired with it?"

"Oh, yeah," her face brightened and she ran off to grab and de-couple her phone. I restarted the news story a second time.

Inanna appeared in the doorway, helplessly looking down at her unfastened jeans.

"Should I do the zipper first, or snap first?"

"Snap first, then zip. Why are we having this conversation?"

I suddenly remembered that the girls had been wearing pull-on shorts and dresses all summer. The fall weather had been late to arrive, and the girls were just coming around to wearing clothes for cooler weather. I suddenly felt sorry that I had been so short with Inanna. I stooped to help her with her jeans.

"Like this," I gently guided her through the motions. "Snap, then zip."

She gave me a big grin. "Mom, can I have a kiss? On the lips?"

I knew what that meant. I gave her a wink, then grabbed my baby pink sheer lip gloss. I smoothed it on my lips and leaned over, puckering for her. She gave me a few pecks on the lips, picking up as much lip gloss as she could.

"There," I said, hoisting her into my arms and pressing our cheeks together. We checked out our reflection in the mirror. "We're practically twins."

She grinned again and skipped off to her bedroom.

"Socks," I called after her. "Don't forget to put on socks."

Morgan appeared in the bathroom almost as soon as Inanna left.

"You know, Mom, I made it all the way to level 80 in Lava Rock Smashers."

I hated video games, but knew that this was Morgan's favorite game. I mustered some real enthusiasm: "That's great! Sounds like you're pretty good at that game."

Morgan prattled on about the game. Apparently, it had something to do with a race against an exploding volcano that involved a bunch of magical lizards and a giant fist that smashes the lava rock. Then something happens that unlocks new levels and lets you buy accessories for your lizard that enhance their powers (Get iridescent feathers for your Bird Lizard! A lightning bolt for Cloud Lizard!).

My hair was a mess. I needed to grab my baseball cap and nearly tripped over Morgan while trying to get to my closet. The radio droned on in the background while Morgan talked about the game. She was saying something about having bought a lightning bolt for Cloud Lizard or a fire blaster for Demon Lizard. I couldn't find the damned cap, and was debating whether I had time to hit my hair with the flat iron before heading out, or if I'd have to pull it into a bun.

"And theeeen I used more points to get a fire blaster for Demon Lizard. A fire blaster!" Morgan was feeling good.

I inhaled sharply. Video game talk was the last thing I wanted to hear this morning. I tried to change the subject. "I thought you wanted to listen to the news."

"Oh, you can turn it off," Morgan said.

"Don't turn it off!" yelled Kali from her room. I yanked my hand from the phone. I was half a second from turning the news report off. I had no idea when Kali had developed superhuman hearing abilities, but it was clear that she could hear our entire conversation.

I sighed and ran my fingers through my hair. My best bet was a messy chignon. It had to be done just right. There was a fine line between looking cool and looking like I'd just rolled out of bed.

"Well, Mira is even better at Lava Rock Smashers than I am." Morgan cocked her head and thought for a moment. "You know, Mom, she's my first best friend. Lillian is my second best friend. Wait, no. Actually, Kim is my second best friend. Lillian is my third."

Here it was: the meat of the conversation. Morgan had been going through some drama with her friends lately. I had tried to help her through it, but it felt like I had only succeeded in doing was re-opening some of my own pre-adolescent battle wounds.

It's funny; Kali hadn't talked about any of this when she was Morgan's age. I sensed that she was one of the stronger personalities in her group of friends. It wasn't until now, at 15, that I was starting to sense her unease. Like me, boys had become her drug of choice. Kali would require an entirely different kind of intervention.

For now, I paused the newscast and turned my attention to Morgan. I swept my hand across her forehead and held her face in my hands. She was such a beautiful child. "Sweetheart, we don't rank people. Certainly not our friends." I kissed the tip of her nose and turned back to the mirror.

"Oh my god, mom!" Kali's disembodied voice wailed from her bedroom.

"I'm talking to Morgan," I called. "I'll turn it on again in a minute."

I brushed my hair back, swept it in one hand and twisted it loosely. I held my hair there for a moment, making sure it fell messily enough to look chic, but not so messy that it looked like I'd done my hair in the dark. It looked good.

"Some friends are fun to do something adventurous with." I pinched several gold bobby pins out of a matchbox-sized tin and spilled them onto the counter. I opened the first pin with my teeth and speared my messy twist to my head. "Know what I mean?" Morgan nodded.

I continued: "Others are great to share a secret with. Other friends are good to study with or to talk to about a book or a movie that you love. But they're all good friends."

I grabbed a hand mirror, checked out my hair from the back and grimaced. Morgan chuckled. I slid a couple more pins into my hair and checked the mirror again.

"Looks good," I decided aloud, then continued: "That's the way it is with friends, or with anyone we love. Just because we like one friend a lot doesn't mean that we like another friend any less."

My stomach dropped as I said those last words. Those words were as true for Morgan as they were for me. Just because I loved Julian didn't mean that I loved Aaron any less.

"Okay, mom. Thanks." Morgan looked thoughtful.

I put a hand on her shoulder and looked at her squarely. "You're a good friend," I said with a little smile.

She smiled back. "I'm glad you're back in town," she replied before heading back to her own room.

I turned to take one last look in the mirror before leaving the room. Shit. Was I cool and sophisticated, or just messy? I couldn't decide.

6.1

FUTURE SELF

LILY LOOKED AT HER WATCH. SHE HAD BOOKED A late flight out of St. Louis, which was further delayed by a thunderstorm. Now, she'd be getting home really late. It was 1am and the flight had just landed. It would take 15 minutes to get to her car and another 30 minutes to drive home. She'd be in bed between 2am and 2:30. She'd have to wake up no later than 6:30 the next day so that she could wash her hair before her 8:30 new business meeting. She sighed. It was only Tuesday. This was a rough way to start the week.

She was mildly comforted by the thought that all of the other business travelers on the flight were in a similar situation. All of them, she was sure, were starting their work week with a delayed flight and little sleep.

Still, she could hardly have found herself in better company. Business travelers were all courteous to one another. There was little glamour in running to catch an early-morning or late-night flight, or in the little indignities that seemed to define air travel. They all seemed to understand that the key to keeping their humanity intact was to be kind to fellow travelers. They held doors for each other, helped one another with bags and charged each other's phones. It was good travel karma.

The passengers filed off of the plane and walked through the empty terminal. Lily smiled and nodded at the man who had been seated next to her on the flight. He nodded and touched his hat before heading toward baggage claim. Other passengers peeled off here and there as they made their way to their destinations. Lily, along with a handful of straggling travelers, took the escalator up and headed down a long corridor to the parking garage elevator. She held the door for four people behind her, finally letting the door slide shut when everyone was on board. She exited the elevator on the 5th floor of the garage with a nod and a thank you to the man who held the door for her.

She felt her body relax when she spotted her car. It was always a relief to see her car when she returned from a trip. Even before she stepped into her apartment, getting into her car felt a little like home. The seat was adjusted just so, and the music she loved was at her fingertips. Lily did a quick scan of the parking lot. There were still lots of cars around despite the hour. She quickened her step as she approached her car. She could hear the footfalls of the two other passengers who exited the elevator behind her. As long as she heard two sets of footsteps and not more, she was fine.

She did her usual scan from afar. There was no one under the car and no one sitting in any of the cars nearby. The coast was clear. She pressed the button on her car remote. The headlights flashed reassuringly as the horn gave a short sound. The interior lights came on. There was no one in the car. She opened the passenger door and put her roller bag on the floor, then walked to the driver's side and got in.

Lily froze. Something was wrong. Everything just felt...off.

There were two cough drops in the cup holder. Those were not hers. A booster seat in the back. How on Earth had she missed that? She didn't have kids. And there was a contrasting color on the dash -- a detail that Lily's car didn't have. She was mortified. This was not her car.

She got out of the car and backed away. She felt a prickly sensation on the back of her neck. Lily looked around and saw a woman close the door to an identical-looking car and back away. The woman walked to the back of the car and checked the license plate. Lily decided to do the same.

"I'm so sorry, but I think I just got in your car," Lily offered as she walked toward her own vehicle.

The woman looked exhausted and still slightly confused. "How did that happen?" she asked with a nervous laugh.

"I don't know." Lily looked down at the remote control in her hand. "Did you...did we unlock our cars at the exact same time?" She could barely believe that it was possible.

"Oh my goodness. Oh, my. I think we did," the woman replied. She was as stunned as Lily was. She wrinkled her nose. "That's so unusual."

"Yeah, and we're both probably exhausted. I know I am," Lily gave her a sympathetic smile. "I didn't even realize that I wasn't in my own car."

"And I was so busy checking out the parking lot to make sure that I was safe...I just didn't notice." The woman laughed and shook her head.

"Me, too!" Lily exclaimed. "Wow, what a night."

They wished other good night and a safe trip home.

The following week, Lily had an early flight to Cincinnati. As she waited in the line that snaked through the security checkpoint, she saw the woman from the parking lot. She, like Lily, was holding a cup of coffee and would have to dump it before going through the security scanners. They were both trying to finish as much of their drink as they could before being forced to throw it away.

Lily waited for a point in the line when they were facing one another, then made eye contact to say hello. Lily saw a flash of recognition in the woman's eyes just before she jerked her head in the other direction and looked away.

Lily felt a surge of embarrassment. What had just happened? She was sure that the woman had recognized her, and she had seemed so friendly just the week before. Besides, this wasn't the way frequent travelers treated one another, even when they didn't know each other. She tried not to think about it, but found that she could think of nothing else.

She didn't know what made her decide to follow the woman. She had more than an hour before her flight, and the woman was in the same terminal. Lily didn't want to seem like a creep, but couldn't square why the woman had gone out of her way to avoid her. She didn't have anything better to do, anyway. She could re-read her meeting materials, or she could follow a fascinating stranger. She decided to follow the stranger.

They disappeared into the airport crowd. She followed the woman, letting her gain some distance. The woman didn't seem to notice. She was in a hurry, and suddenly started rubbing and blotting her jacket with a tissue she produced from her pocket. Lily imagined that she was rushing to make her flight after a harried morning wrangling kids. After all, the woman had a booster seat in the back of her car. She imagined the woman trying to leave home, her child clinging to her, smudging syrup or applesauce on her suit.

The woman slowed and approached a gate. Lily settled into a seat across the corridor and tried to look busy. The woman looked around and locked eyes with a man who looked like he was her own age. Lily was a little surprised. The two didn't look like colleagues. He was wearing sandals and a polo shirt, and looked like he was a few weeks overdue for a haircut. Lily wondered for a moment if the man was her son, but quickly rejected the thought. The woman couldn't have been older than 45, she guessed. It was certainly a possibility, but it didn't seem likely.

The woman sat next to him, and he handed her a fresh cup of coffee. Lily briefly cursed her decision to the follow the woman instead of getting a new, hot cup of coffee. It was time to go. This was silly.

She gave them one last look before getting up. His hand was still on the coffee cup, and her hand was caressing his. They were gazing into each other's eyes.

"I'll be damned," she muttered to herself. "Those two are sleeping together."

Lily forgot about getting coffee.

The couple exchanged flirtatious glances for a few minutes, then got up to leave. They wandered slowly, looking around. Lily followed them. At this point, she felt compelled to. The pair ducked behind a column and disappeared from her line of sight. Lily kept walking. She would have to walk past the column and look backward to see them.

Once she was past the column, she held her breath and

turned to look. The two were kissing intensely, his hand up the back of her shirt and his groin pressed into her. The woman opened her eyes for a moment and saw Lily. Startled, she pushed her lover away, smoothing her clothes. Lily looked away, too, her ears burning. The woman had definitely recognized her. This, she thought, was why she had avoided Lily in the security line.

Later on the plane, she turned the scene over and over in her mind. She had caught the woman with a man who was not her husband. She felt a broad sense of embarrassment, and an acute stab of shame that she had followed the woman and intruded on her indiscretion. She wished that she could unsee what she had seen. She gazed out of the window at the patchwork-quilt landscape and wondered how many other scenes like the one she had just seen were playing out below.

6.2

THROUGH THE LOOKING-GLASS

EVERYTHING REMINDED ME OF JULIAN.

I wondered if this had been part of his plan all along. I had done everything possible to forget him, and had met and married a wonderful man. Then, he re-appeared out of practically nowhere, saying all of the things that I had imagined him saying as I consoled myself over the grief of our estrangement. He was so sorry, he said. He needed another chance, he said, to show me how much he loves being with me. He wasn't going to let me go again. Who knew what that meant since we were both married, but it was everything I had wanted to hear for so long.

In this new, twisted version of our relationship, he would bombard me with adoration then disappear for weeks on end. I was starting to feel desperate. Our communication was thinning out. Suddenly, he just wasn't available when I needed to hear his voice. I cursed myself for having deleted his text messages. I had done it to avoid getting caught, but at that moment, I desperately wanted to read and re-read them to reassure me that his feelings for me made our communication gaps insignificant. Without those messages, the gaps yawned between us, revealing black, unending depths.

I recognized this as our old pattern. In fact, I had never felt so lonely as when I was with him. I needed to do something to shake this feeling.

It was a gorgeous day for driving. I put on my big oval sunglasses and shook my hair out of a ponytail. I checked myself in the mirror at a red light, pressing my lips together. No, I didn't need more lip color. I looked great.

I flipped the air conditioning off, let the windows all the way down and opened the sunroof. I was getting on the highway, and a day like this called for riding with the windows down and the music up.

Aaron had recognized my mood as soon as I declared that I was going out.

"Coming back?" he asked.

I laughed as I grabbed my keys. I needed somewhere to put my big, wild energy.

"Okay," he said, turning back to the football game. "Just let me know if you'll be back in time for dinner or if the girls and I should get something on our own."

The day crackled with the brilliant beauty of autumn. The electric blue sky was hung with low, overstuffed clouds that dappled the ground with intermittent shade. I pressed the accelerator and felt a rush as the car's engine responded to my command. The car opened up, reaching 90 miles per hour with ease. I loved my car; it was like my avatar. And sometimes, I reasoned, it needed a break from shuttling the girls to school. After all, it was a Porsche. The opening guitar scream of The System's

Don't Disturb This Groove tore into the air. It was perfect. I belted the lyrics into the wind while my hair whipped around me.

I passed a beautiful black Mustang on my right. The driver, a dark-haired man with sunglasses, looked like he was enjoying a drive just like I was. We exchanged a look. He revved his engine and pulled ahead, then changed lanes so that he was ahead of me. He looked in the rear view mirror and waved. I smiled, still singing. I tailed him for about a mile, then shifted lanes and punched the gas. I sailed past him, then changed lanes again so that I was in front again. I blew him a kiss in the rear view mirror. He laughed.

I had left home without a destination. But in truth, there was nowhere to go. I decided to go to the nearest mall. I had heard that there was a good one nearby. The mall near my home was where I normally went when I needed to escape. It took the first few visits, though, to get over a slight feeling of deja vu. Something about the place was oddly familiar, though I was certain that I hadn't been there before. Something about the particular mix of stores, the meandering indoor landscaping, the fountains in the light-filled central atrium, even the footprint of the mall itself, haunted me. After a few weeks, I figured out what made the experience so strange. It was a sister property to the mall near our New Jersey home. Same stores, same trees, same fountains, same developer. I had moved 1,000 miles across the country just to find the same mall. I felt relieved to have figured it out, but crushed by what I could only describe as a kind of doom. I felt I had traded one gilded cage for another. For a long time, I wondered if anyone else could see the bars.

I pulled off at the next exit and pulled out my phone for directions, then made my way to Royal Pines mall. I felt hopeful.

Maybe this one would feel different from the rest.

So, there I was, at Royal Pines. It was beautiful. Then again, all of the upscale malls were. Like the others, the layout was lovely, with natural light, fountains and landscaping. It was a glorified walking path, anchored with expensive department stores. Like the rest of them, it contained the requisite combination of Victoria's Secret, Lululemon and Williams-Sonoma stores. Well, at least it was a good place to take a walk.

My phone rang. It was Julian.

"Hi there, little lady," he teased.

"Hey."

"What's going on?"

"Nothing much. I'm just at the mall, enjoying some alone time," I sighed.

"Oh, of course," he snarked. "You're probably doing all kinds of damage. I know how you ladies love to shop."

I didn't know where to begin with that comment. I considered hanging up and blaming it on a poor connection.

"So...can you talk?" He sounded hopeful.

"I'm meeting one of my friends in about half an hour, but I can still talk," I lied.

I didn't have plans to meet anyone. This really was my my time alone. But Julian and I had fewer and fewer chances to talk to each other lately. I had to take what I could get.

I let Julian tell me about his week. I didn't feel very talkative, so it felt fine to let him chat. He noticed.

"I'm doing all of the talking here," he said. "Tell me what's going on in your world."

"Well...nothing, really."

It felt like the truth. I felt like I was on an invisible hamster wheel of school, dinner plans and clean-up duty, punctuated by obligatory kids' birthday parties. It was the reason why I was currently walking the mall -- to escape a feeling of great, yawning nothingness.

"You're holding back. I hate it when you hold back parts of yourself from me." Julian surprised me with his challenge to my silence.

"Is that what I'm doing? I certainly didn't mean to hold back." I really didn't think that I was withholding anything.

"That's what it feels like to me," he answered.

I sucked in a deep breath and scraped my brain for an answer. "Well," I started, "We're going to Toronto with the girls in about a month."

"That'll be great! Hey, remember, I lived there for a while. I can tell you all kinds of interesting things to do while you're there," he gushed. His voice then fell. "Actually, I can't. All I ever do is work. I never actually got out and enjoyed the city, even when I lived there."

I tried to encourage him. "Well, I don't need to know about the big, exciting things. Those are the kinds of things that I can read about, anyway. Tell me...I don't know, tell me what restaurants you and your wife liked most."

Your wife. It was a small dig that I'm not even sure he noticed. When I was feeling annoyed, I'd say that instead of her name. It was just a little poke to remind him how I feel about being a side piece.

"Oh, Jessica? She hated it there," he drew out the word hate to emphasize the point.

"Hated it? Why? Who hates living in Toronto?"

"Well, when we moved there, she had just had our first baby. She didn't have any friends or family there, and she said it was really hard to meet people. She wasn't working, so she was at home with the baby, well, babies once our second was born. Anyway, she hated it."

"Hmph," I replied.

He had just told me that story without a trace of irony. It was like he hadn't heard any of the things I told him about being dragged across the country, far from family, friends and the career I'd built. And, by his own admission, he works all the time. It was like he didn't even see his role in his wife's isolation.

His voice brightened. "But now, she's glad to be living in Connecticut because she's back at work, and we have a nanny who's amazing with the kids." He changed the subject. "Speaking of travel, I'll be in Indianapolis four weeks from today. Can you meet me there?"

I hesitated. "I'll have to see. I have to check my schedule. Right now, I can't really see beyond the Toronto trip." It was true. There was laundry and packing and itineraries and food and hotels and unpacking and more laundry to think about.

"We had dinner with one of my colleagues and his new wife last night," he said.

"Mmmhmm," I replied.

"They just got married a few months ago. It's his second marriage. Anyway, she's a younger woman. She's some kind of beauty queen. She did beauty pageants or something -- like, maybe she's a former Miss Mexico. Anyway, she is gorgeous. She is an insanely beautiful woman."

I toyed with different ways to end the conversation. I came here to spend some time alone, and the last thing I wanted to hear was Julian going on about how beautiful some other woman was.

"She doesn't work. So, every night when he comes home, she's just at home, waiting for him. That's pretty great, don't you think?"

"If that's what you're into, then sure." I was noncommittal.

"Do you think you could do that?"

"I'm not sure what you mean," I said. I wasn't going to make this easy for him.

"Do you think you could -- I mean, could you be the kind of wife that's just at home, waiting for your man?"

"I don't think it's that simple." I really didn't want to have this conversation.

"Seriously, is that something you'd be willing to do if we were together?"

I sighed. "Well, if there were no kids involved, maybe. And I love to cook, but if that were my job, I wouldn't like it very much. I do enough of that now. I'm constantly having to figure out what to cook for the girls every day, several times a day."

I thought about it. What Julian was proposing was very different from the actual lives of women I knew. I was sure that some of their husbands, like Julian, imagined that their wives just sat around all day like some pet, waiting for them to get home.

"I would need something to occupy my time," I continued. "Like, maybe I'd learn a couple of languages. And I'd definitely have to work out. And I would probably spend a lot of time helping out with causes that I really like. But if I were to do all of those things, it's very likely that I wouldn't be home, ready to receive you the minute you get there."

"So, that's something that you'd be willing to do?" He

wasn't getting my point. I gave up.

"Yes, I guess. Maybe." I changed the subject. "Hey, my girlfriend just showed up. She's actually a bit early. I'll talk to you later, okay?"

"That's cool. You seem to be in a strange mood today, anyway."

I resisted the urge to smash my phone on the floor. I couldn't do that. The phone was too expensive.

* * *

We sat on opposite sides of the loveseat in Julian's Indianapolis hotel room, trying to create as much distance between us as the two-cushion seat would allow. "Are you breaking up with me?" Julian asked.

I hated him for making me say it. "Well, it's just that we can't keep doing this. *I* can't keep doing it." I had told him that the relationship felt like another failure; that I was worried that we hardly ever talk anymore; that I'm not comfortable sleeping with someone I barely talk to.

He looked at his hands in his lap and shook his head slowly. "You really are the only real friend that I have; the only person who I can really talk to."

I didn't know how to answer. I didn't know how to tell him that I felt abandoned by the lack of communication, and that a real friend wouldn't do that to me. Instead, I let the silence hang between us for a while.

"Well," I said, standing up and looking around for my bag, "I should go."

"Where will you go?" he asked. "It's almost midnight."

"No, it's not. It's --" I checked my phone. "Shit. It's after 11:00." I had lost track of time while we talked.

"Leave in the morning," he said softly. "Don't go out tonight."

I put on my best I-won't-hear-another-word-about-it voice. "I'm an adult," I clipped. "I'll be just fine." Surely I could find a hotel with a vacancy somewhere. Then I remembered that there were two big conferences and a concert that were happening at the same time. I worried about where I would stay. I thought about sleeping in my car. All I knew was that I didn't want to say here. If I couldn't find a hotel, I'd sleep in my car. I had never done that before, and didn't know where I could do it safely, but I refused to let Julian know that.

"Come on. It's late and you'll never find a place to stay. It was almost impossible for me to get this room," he said, vaguely gesturing at the beige-and-gray motif around us. "I need to make sure you're safe. I don't want you running around town trying to find a place to stay. Sleep here, with me. Please. Leave in the morning, when it's safer for you to get on the road."

I gave in. I was exhausted from our talk, anyway. And Julian was right: it would have been very hard to find a hotel room. I had looked for one before coming here. It was going to be my escape plan. None of the hotels I liked were available. Once I got here, I didn't have the nerve to begin the conversation with Julian until late in the evening. So there I was, stuck in a hotel room with the man who I had just dumped.

We undressed wordlessly, each going into the bathroom to disrobe in private. We gave each other wide berth and offered each other stilted courtesies as we made our way to bed. He offered to sleep on the loveseat.

"Of course you won't sleep on that thing," I tutted. "There's plenty of room right here."

I folded the covers back on one side of the bed and gestured, offering it to him. It felt as benign as holding the door for a stranger. He climbed into bed and we wished each other good night.

My thoughts raced. I lay on my back and closed my eyes, hoping that the stillness of my body would help calm my mind. It was useless.

You should have slept in your fucking car. This is pathetic. You think you're a grown-up because you can sleep with him without "sleeping" with him? Fine. But you know you want him. He's right there!

I looked to my left and saw Julian lying as still as I was, eyes closed. There was nearly a foot of space between us, but I felt our old familiar electricity sparking again. I squeezed my eyes shut and tried to quiet my inner voice.

Rub his chest. Stroke his hair. Tell him you're sorry. Admit that you want him. Give him a kiss on the cheek.

That was it. I'd give him a kiss on the cheek. If he was asleep, it wouldn't wake him. If he was, I could pretend that it was nothing; just a harmless little kiss.

I rolled onto my side and leaned in to kiss him, careful to bring my face close to his without closing the distance between our bodies. At the last moment, I shifted and planted the kiss on his lips. "Good night," I whispered. We had already wished each other good night, but I couldn't think of anything else to say.

In a flash, Julian threw me on my back and pulled my pajama pants off. He flung them across the room and dove into me. He tossed my legs over his shoulders, pinning me to the bed, and banged into me. I was aware that I was grunting. It wasn't a sexy moan, but an involuntary sound made possible by the position where he held me, his vigorous thrusting and my inability to move. I tried to look at his face. He was fucking like I wasn't even there. There was no eye contact, no kiss, no sign of intimacy. It was strange that even this felt good. Then again, he always felt good inside me. I just needed him to look at me. I craned my head toward his, willing him to make eye contact. He refused.

I think this is hate fucking. I'm being hate fucked!

He moved to his knees, still thrusting into me, and grabbed my ankles tightly, pushing my knees to my shoulders. I could hardly breathe. Holding my foot aloft, he put my toes into his mouth, fondling them with his tongue while he pounded me. I melted into pleasure, eyes rolling. He brought my other foot close to his face, then raked his teeth along the ball of my foot. It was more than I could stand. I climaxed, nearly screaming as his thrusts grew harder and faster. He climaxed with me, still thrusting. He finished and put both of my legs to one side, then rolled off of me to the other side. He lay on his side with his back to me, panting.

I lay on my back and stared at the ceiling. A laugh bubbled from deep in my belly. I languished in it, laughing as heartily as my spent body allowed. Julian shot a morose look at me over his shoulder.

"That was fantastic," I grinned. "You are always, always fantastic."

His eyes left my face and went to the ceiling. He rolled onto his back and his chest heaved with a giant sigh. "I can't believe it. I will always want you. Even when..." he trailed off and shook his head, still staring at the ceiling.

My phone pinged. Normally, I wouldn't answer a text at a moment like this, but I had just been hate fucked. I didn't care about being polite anymore.

```
•••  Sprint LTE    12:10 AM      59%
   < Messages   ICE Aaron         Details

   Hey, Sexy.

   I can't sleep...Feel like
   making a one-handed
   call to your husband?




   📷  iMessage                    Send
```

I gave a short laugh and cradled the phone so that Julian couldn't see the screen. The "one-handed call" that Aaron suggested was our code for phone sex. This was surreal.

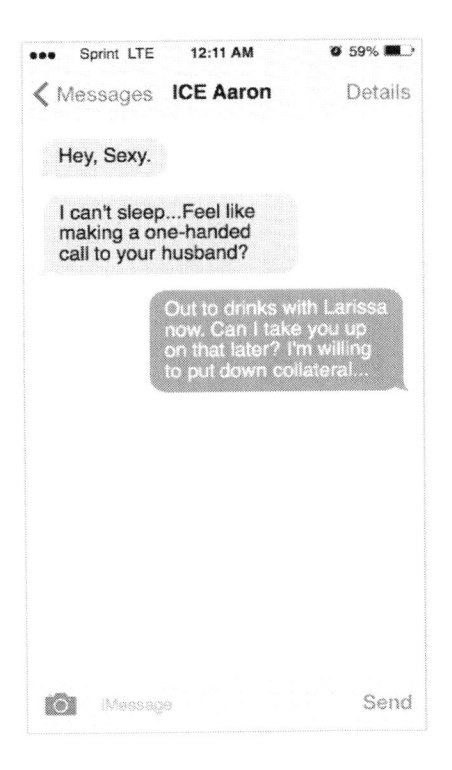

> **Sprint LTE** 12:11 AM 59%
>
> ‹ Messages **ICE Aaron** Details
>
> Hey, Sexy.
>
> I can't sleep...Feel like making a one-handed call to your husband?
>
> Out to drinks with Larissa now. Can I take you up on that later? I'm willing to put down collateral...
>
> iMessage Send

"I'll be right back," I said. The bathroom was on Julian's side of the room. I got up, taking care to exit at the foot of the bed so that I wouldn't bump him, and hurried inside. I flipped on the light, took a close-up selfie of my breasts and sent it to Aaron. My phone pinged again as Aaron sent me a string of emoji. I laughed out loud at his silly reply.

"What's going on?" Julian asked.

"Nothing. It's just Aaron," I shrugged. I put my phone on mute and placed it on the bedside table before climbing into bed again. The phone buzzed and vibrated for a few moments, then stopped.

"I can't believe it. I feel jealous of your husband." Julian looked genuinely miserable.

"I am so, so sorry. I really don't want you to feel bad." I understood how he felt. "This is bad for both of us." I shook my head. "You and I have never not been dysfunctional. I would love to try this," I said, gesturing back and forth between him and me, "when we can do it in the open; when we can let the world know that we're together. Until then, we should probably just stop."

I was saying the right words but didn't really want to leave. I made myself stand. He moved in front of me gently and kissed me lightly on the lips, then across my face and neck. There was no sound except that of our breath. I took half a step and he kneeled in front of me, pushing my pants down past my hips and kissing my stomach and the top of my mound. I felt myself letting go. His tongue traced down until it teased just above my clitoris. His breath was hot against my skin.

I pushed his shoulders away gently, pulling my hips backward to create some space between us. He looked up at me, puzzled. "Why won't you let me please you that way?" he asked.

I didn't know how to explain how strange it was the last time he had gone down on me. Back in college, he was a master of bringing me pleasure orally. Now, it was like he had been re-calibrated for another woman's body. His wife's body.

I decided to dodge the question. "I guess I'm just not ready right now"

He gave me a curious look, then stood and stepped out of the way.

* * *

"Pull yourself together," I muttered to myself. I had been

thinking about the affair for most of the flight but didn't feel like I had come to a resolution

"That's it. I'm going to make a list."

Whenever I felt uncertain or out of control, I turned to list-making. It was a small way to assert control over my world when things got chaotic. The man in the aisle seat glanced in my direction and smiled tightly. I was pretty sure that the flight noise had masked what I said, but it probably didn't disguise the fact that I had been distracted for much of the flight and was now muttering to myself. I didn't care. I had bigger things to worry about. I grabbed my cocktail napkin and found a pen at the bottom of my purse.

THE RULES

I scrawled the words in all caps at the top of the napkin and underlined it, hard. The napkin tore a bit where I had underlined the words. I smoothed the napkin and wrote down the first rule.

1: CALM THE FUCK DOWN.

This was a direct command to me. My relationship with Julian was like an old, abandoned campsite. We had never really extinguished the fire. All it took was the right set of circumstances to make a few hot embers ignite into a roaring forest fire. I had to control myself. Julian and I had missed our chance at love. We were done. And truthfully, my life was much better with Aaron.

I exhaled. I felt a little better already.

2: HE IS NOT YOUR HUSBAND.

Well, that much was clear. As thrilling as it was to have Julian around again, it was obvious that he was nothing like Aaron. I didn't even need the same things from them. Aaron was my partner -- my friend, lover and confidant. It was harder to say what Julian was to me. Maybe it was less about who he was than how he made me feel. I couldn't quite put my finger on it, except to say that he seemed to remind me of the person I used to be. My husband was kind and funny and warm and was all of the things I had ever said I wanted in a husband. And Julian...well, he made me feel good. Very good. Except when he didn't.

"He is not your husband," I muttered to myself. It felt kind of thrilling to say the words aloud. I repeated them, a little louder this time. "Julian is not your husband." The man in the next seat cleared his throat. I put my pen to the little napkin again:

3: DON'T GET EMOTIONALLY INVOLVED.

I looked at that one for a while. I needed something stronger. I scrawled the next thought in all caps:

3: FUCK YOUR FEELINGS!!!

That felt right. I sat up straight for a moment and closed my eyes. The words bounced around my head. Yeah, that's what I needed. A reminder -- a strong reminder -- that this wasn't a relationship. It didn't even meet my minimum acceptable standards. Yeah, I have standards! I opened my eyes, suddenly embarrassed. I wasn't quite sure whether I had said that out loud. The man in the next seat had craned his neck to get a look at my little napkin. I lay my hand flat over my scrawl, looked out of the window and pretended not to notice that he had been looking.

I couldn't possibly expect the affair with Julian to go anywhere. But he was the one who had brought up getting married. I shook my head at the thought. They were the right words, but they were 20 years too late. We had missed our chance. Point 3 was as much for Julian as it was for me. I lifted my palm so that the napkin was still shielded from prying eyes and crossed out the first four words. This was about feelings. And engaging with feelings would only make the last point even harder. I took a deep breath and penned the last point:

4: THIS WILL END.

I looked at the words for a while. They seemed so simple. They were deceptively so. The ending would almost certainly be the most complicated part, and someone would definitely get hurt. The best scenario would be that Julian and I absorbed the pain of our breakup on our own. It would be unfair to let Aaron or Jessica or any of our kids know about it. I traced and re-traced the letters w-i-l-l four times, then underlined the word until the tip of the pen tore through the napkin. The pen left a mark on the tray table. I rubbed at the mark, then examined the smudge that had transferred to my fingertip. A black mark that wouldn't go away.

I was miserable. List-making normally made me feel better, but putting these four points on paper seemed to suck the energy from me. I slumped in my seat and stared at the napkin for what felt like a long time.

I felt eyes on me. The man sitting nearest me was staring openly, eyes widened. I looked at the napkin, ink-smeared with too-heavy writing and crossed-out words. The last two points jumped out at me: FUCK YOUR FEELINGS!!! and THIS WILL END. I looked back at his face. He looked like he wanted to jump out of his seat.

I turned the napkin over, stretched out my legs and pretended to sleep.

* * *

Aaron snuggled close to me in the dark. "As I recall, you put down collateral on some grown-up time last night," he said suggestively.

"Did that selfie help you out at all?" I batted my eyes at him.

"I had fun with it, for sure. I was just hoping to have the real thing tonight."

Our kisses turned into slow, lazy lovemaking. It was wonderful. Suddenly, Aaron shifted gears. He was energetic; enthusiastic. His excitement turned me on. He rolled me onto my back and scooped one arm under each of my knees. He shifted again, putting my knees over his shoulders, and thrust into me. I looked up at him. His face was mostly shadowed. He was clearly enjoying this position. I didn't have much mobility with my legs so far back, so I tilted my hips to help him out. His moans told me that he liked what I was doing. He suddenly stopped thrusting and got on his knees. He grabbed my ankles, pulled both feet to his face and inhaled deeply. Then he raked the tips of my toes with his teeth.

I shuddered and momentarily lost track of everything. Was this today or yesterday? Was I at home or in a hotel room? Was I having sex with Aaron or Julian? I strained against the darkness to see the face that hovered above me. I couldn't make out his face. I panicked for a moment, and grasped at the sheets. They were my sheets. I was at home, in my own bed, making love to my own husband.

Was Aaron signaling that he knew about my affair with Julian? No, that didn't make sense. Even if he did know, there's no way that he'd know about the specific position that Julian and I had enjoyed just the day before: knees over shoulders, feet at his face. I felt deeply unsettled. It wasn't my imagination or a fantasy; I had actually confused my own husband with Julian while we were in the act. In that moment, it seemed clear: I had to to stop this madness with Julian.

I lay on my side with Aaron curled behind me, face buried in my hair. His breathing had slowed and deepened. He was asleep. I could feel the moist warmth of his breath at the back of my head. I relaxed and thought about my situation.

I've heard it said that each person in the world has something to teach you, and that life lessons will repeat themselves until they've been learned. I wondered what lesson Julian was supposed to teach me, and why the hell I hadn't learned it yet.

Out of nowhere, the thought hit me: Maybe there was no grand lesson to be learned here. Maybe Julian's only purpose was to ruin my life. I lay as still as I could, unblinking, in the dark.

7.1

THE GO-TO

SHE WAS ON HER WAY TO HER SUMMER INTERNSHIP when she met Mark. He had chocolate skin and a thick black mustache. He was short, which she didn't normally like, but his incongruously had tickled her to the base of her spine when he asked her name. Mark was self-assured. Forward. His attention was only for her, as if she were the last woman alive. It was as if he knew something, and was confident that she would want to know it, too. By the time she recognized what was happening, she had accepted his proposal for a date. There was no other way to respond to him.

Lily was aware that the balance had tipped against her, but she kind of liked it. Mark was in control. It felt heady and a little dangerous. She had always had a strong sense of the effect she had on the men she met. She loved that she made them a bit nervous, stumbling adorably as they figured out how to talk to her. This was entirely different. She thought about him all afternoon and evening. He was so...dominant. She wasn't sure how she felt about the fact that she found it so sexy.

He had invited her to his place. He was going to cook dinner and they'd spend the evening in. Oddly, Mark's house looked like an old woman's home. Like maybe it had been his grandmother's house. He made no attempt to explain the decor. Something about about that made her feel wildly self-conscious. This was clearly not her script. It was his.

Her skin prickled as she became aware of a large presence behind her. She turned to find herself practically face-to-face with a very tall dog. This dog seemed to understand personal space. Rather than nosing its way to her, it stood with dispassionate eyes and a slightly on-guard posture about five feet away.

"That's a wolf," he told her. "Only 10 percent dog. Just enough to make it legal to have her."

"Oh, cool." Lily tried to sound like a wolf-dog in an old-lady house was the most normal thing in the world.

Wolf-dog glided to Mark and sat next to him, facing Lily. She was great and gray with coarse fur that stood out from her neck. She regarded Lily coolly. Mark gave a hand signal and the beast disappeared. She wove through the doilied furniture as large as a pony and as soundlessly as a housecat. There was none of the usual floppy, mouth-breathing jangling of a normal pet dog.

Mark uncorked a bottle of wine. "It's a Beaujolais," he said, pouring two glasses and handing her the first one.

She took it. Sounded French. Sounded fine. She didn't know much about wine, but had studied enough French to recognize a few varietals. She took the glass and swirled the deep burgundy liquid around the bowl before putting it to her lips. It went down like velvet. This guy was good. She felt herself beginning to relax.

Mark's virtuosity in the kitchen was impressive. Lily settled into her glass of wine, content to watch him move. He shimmied to the counter; arched his back to get a glance of something in a high cabinet; held the refrigerator door ajar with the tips of his outstretched fingers while rinsing his knife in the sink. His command of the space was exquisite.

He cut the ends off of a handful of asparagus stalks. "Do you like asparagus?" It was less a question than a declaration of intent.

Lily nodded as she swallowed a sip of wine. She didn't like asparagus enough to eat it on a first date. For Lily, asparagus pee was right up there with garlic breath. She normally avoided it until she was very comfortable with the relationship.

After another glass of wine, Mark presented a beautiful ribeye steak with a crispy sear. Lily cut into it and speared a piece. It was a picture-perfect rare, its light char set off by a gorgeous bright red center.

"Wow," she purred. "That looks gorgeous."

She preferred her steak cooked medium. He hadn't asked.

Mark insisted on clearing the plates on his own. They chatted as he washed the dishes and put everything away. Wolf-dog reappeared, sitting precisely at the corner of the kitchen tile. Cara noted that the dog was not actually in the kitchen. This was clearly an arrangement that Mark and his dog had established long before.

Mark tossed a few scraps of steak toward the animal, which snatched them out of midair with a dry snap of her jaws. This time, Lily nearly missed the small hand gesture that made the beast evaporate into the dark of the living room.

Mark dried the last few dishes and wiped his hands. He looked at Lily for what seemed like a long few minutes. He then stood and reached across the counter for her hand. "Come with me," he said. He led her directly to the bedroom.

There were framed photos of a beautiful woman all over the room. Like the rest of the decor, Mark made no attempt to explain what it was about.

What the absolute fuck is going on here? The voice in her head screamed.

"Ummm, who's that?" she managed. She was trying to sound calm.

Mark picked up one of the pictures by the corner of the frame, tilting it toward him to gaze at it full on.

"That's my wife," he said, then looked at Lily steadily.

"You didn't say anything about being married..." she started.

"My girl; my sweetheart; that's my heart," he interrupted, cutting her off. He was now gazing at another picture, this one of him in the driver's seat of a car, looking gorgeous in a pair of black aviator sunglasses. His girlfriend was sitting in the passenger seat, out of frame. Their hands are clasped, and he's kissing the back of her fingers, looking elated. "That's the woman I'm going to marry."

The voice in Lily's head went into overdrive.

Well, this is some shit. I am done with this crazy date. He's called that woman his fucking wife.... She took another look at the photo on the bedside table and felt her stomach muscles relax. *Well, I wanted to know what it would feel like to let this guy take control, and here I am. I guess the shrine to his so-called wife is no crazier than the granny house or the wolf-dog. Fuck it. I'm in.*

Lily closed her eyes and nodded faintly. Mark planted kisses on her eyelids, then moved to her neck and shoulders. Her skin prickled, this time from his moustache.

He stepped back and commanded her to undress, telling her which item of clothing to remove and when; chastising her when she removed an article without his explicit instruction. He was maddeningly calm. Lily couldn't help thinking that Mark was the hottest thing that had happened to her in a while. She was happy to play along.

She stood before him, naked. He licked his lips, casting a long look at her body. Lily felt deeply uncomfortable. This open assessment of her nakedness felt strangely distant. It felt like a test of endurance to let him look at her like this.

He closed the distance between them, kissing her shoulder then guiding her to the floor. He knelt between her knees and let her watch him as he pulled his shirt over his head. His muscles were tight knots along his arms, legs and back. She smiled a bit, letting her eyes sweep over his body.

After she had taken him in visually, Mark locked eyes with her. Holding her gaze as if by command, he unbuckled his belt. Was it her imagination, or had time slowed down? He unbuttoned his jeans and unzipped his pants as if in slow motion. Lily was dying to know what was inside those jeans, and Mark was intentionally teasing her. She didn't dare look away from his gaze. He would tell her when she could look.

Mark interrupted his strip tease. He smoothly dove between her legs, tongue lapping gently, then probing, then sucking lightly at her clit. He brought her close twice, intentionally slowing down before she could reach orgasm. He would tell her when she could cum.

He guided her to the bed, then fished through the bedside table. He produced a long velvet cord and stretched it before him in both hands. It was another statement of intent. Lily raised an eyebrow, indicating something like approval.

Mark tied her left wrist to the bedpost. That seemed fine. The tie felt okay on her right wrist, too. Not too tight. Her arms were splayed apart, but she didn't feel uncomfortable with what was happening. Control was clearly Mark's game. At least this was interesting. She pushed all thoughts of grandmothers and girlfriend-wives out of her mind and instead concerned herself with what would happen next.

Mark bound her ankles. She was spread-eagle on the bed. This was not something she would ever have done before, but Mark was so in control. It seemed natural to follow him. Her thoughts suddenly went to the wolf-dog. Here was a creature that was 90% wild but still let Mark control everything. In this moment, tied to the bed with her arms and legs splayed apart, she felt like she understood.

Mark went back to work, slowly circling her clit with the tip of his tongue. He watched her body writhe. He still hadn't taken his jeans off. He languished, running his tongue up and down her slit. He alternated with kisses to her lips, which had engorged with arousal. He wasn't going to let her climax, and she knew it. There was no point begging. She relaxed and let him play with her reactions.

He slowed to a stop and rose to his feet. He pushed his jeans down past his hips, then reached down to pull them off of his ankles. He was wearing white socks.

Mark's erection was massive.

Lily had only seen anything like it in porn. She had heard about certain actors who use a prosthetic to appear larger, but what stood before her was was no fake. The large penises she had experienced were still quite normal. This was certainly not. She started to worry. Her mind flashed to the woman whose photos decorated the room. She wondered what kind of freak of nature she was. Maybe Mark and his "wife" were meant to be together, after all.

Mark climbed onto the bed, knees just under each of her armpits. His penis thumped against her chin. She licked the underside of the head, watching him. He was watching her. She took as much of him into her mouth as she could from that position. She closed her eyes and imagined unhinging her jaw like a snake. She relaxed her throat, trying not to gag. Her lips stretched ridiculously around his girth. She could only take a few inches of him into her mouth, but she did her best to slicken those few inches. The point of this blow job was lubrication. Mark repositioned himself between her knees.

"This is going to hurt," he said, positioning himself for entry.

Without waiting for her reaction, he pushed into her in one long, merciless thrust. Lily refused to vocalize her pain. She felt her flesh stretch to take him in. It felt like her insides had shifted to make room for him. He was so hard and so large; it was only the heat from his engorged penis that reminded her that it was part of another person. As Mark pulled out to thrust again, deeper and harder, she felt the micro-tears in her skin. This time as he pushed inside her, it stung, and she squeezed back tears. Her only hope was to try to relax and hope that her body would adjust to him.

The pain subsided to a simmering discomfort as Mark thrust himself into her again and again. He wasn't exactly rough, but he didn't have to be. He was simply too much. Lily thought she felt the beginnings of something deep inside, but all of her focus was on relaxing her own body and accommodating Mark.

Her orgasm caught her by surprise. It came in wave after wave. Her body, already stretched to its limits, was now clenching beyond her control around Mark. The sensation was more than she could stand. She whimpered, and tears rolled down the sides of her face.

In the future, that evening with Mark would be Lily's go-to fantasy scene. All she had to do was imagine him with his white socks and that massive erection, promising to hurt her and following through. That was always enough to send her over the edge.

7.2

MUTUALLY-ASSURED DESTRUCTION

I HAD AN IDEA. I WAS FEELING SEXY AND RECKLESS, so why not?

I threw a blanket on my bed and changed into a slinky pink lace bra and matching panties with a peek-a-boo cutout at the rear waistband that showcased my cleavage. I took selfies, reclining on the bed with my eyes closed, mouth open just so and fingers trailing suggestively. I changed again, this time into a black cupless bra and matching thong. This time, I arched my back to get a good shot, the black triangle of the bra giving me just a bit of support from below and laying taut against my skin. My breasts swelled roundly out of the triangle openings, and my nipples had contracted to taut brown nubs, standing on edge at the tips of my breasts. I sucked in my stomach and shot from below to make them look extra sexy. I took a quick look at what I had shot so far.

Damn, I look pretty good! I'm having fun!

Next, I changed into a bra with what looked like a double cup, a black demi cup that would have revealed my nipples were it not for a gauzy inner layer, pleated cleverly for maximum opacity.

This bra also had a matching pair of panties.

Let's see...I have to change it up to keep things interesting....

I got on my knees and looked into the camera, squeezing my breasts together with my camera arm for maximum cleavage and dipping the other hand into my panties. I winked at the camera and shot.

Perfect. Next shot!

I lay on my stomach and flipped my hair, looking up into the camera while getting as much of my backside into the shot as possible. The idea was to do a body shot, but I couldn't quite manage it.

Doesn't matter. As long as my face and ass are in the shot, it's good.

I checked again. My butt was a bit dimpled, but what the hell. I liked what I saw. I was having a blast.

For the final photos, I grabbed a gauzy white t-shirt and threw it on over my naked body. I knew what I was going for; I'd just have to be careful not to drop my phone in the shower. I wet myself down, including my hair and all, taking special care to wet the t-shirt so that it clung to my skin. I snapped a few photos. This, I thought, was the sexiest of the bunch. The t-shirt clung to my body, creasing seductively over every curve. It revealed everything, concealed practically nothing, and yet still enhanced my body.

Water ran in warm rivulets over the gauzy fabric, which was its own kind of seduction. The slick of the water, the cling of the wet shirt, the billowing steam, the impulsive photo shoot...they all swirled together into a heady brew. I felt like a goddess, bestowing one of my many gifts on my lover. And there was one more gift to give.

I found the voice recorder on my phone and put the

device on a ledge away from the shower's spray. I dipped two fingers into my mouth and fondled them with my tongue. I could feel the sensation from my tongue on my fingertips with the sharpened senses of arousal. I sat on the shower bench and dipped my slickened fingers into my vagina. I dipped and probed, then pressed my fingers against the thickened mound of tissue on the front wall -- my G spot. I played there for a bit, pressing and massaging it. I felt myself relax involuntarily, and I moistened inside.

I pulled my fingers out slowly, the walls of my vagina clutching my fingers involuntarily. I focused my slickened fingertips on my clit, which had become sensitive and engorged from the arousal. I touched it lightly and gasped. The direct touch elicited something like pain. It was too intense. I couldn't touch it directly. That was a good sign.

Settling my fingertips on either side of my clit, I rubbed up and down. Slowly at first, I worked it indirectly, making myself moan. I moved my fingers to the top of my clit, moving faster now, but still without directly touching it. My heartbeat drummed in my ears and I was flying now, overtaken by pure sensation.

I could feel the beginnings of an orgasm. It inched closer, like a roller coaster creeping tantalizingly to its highest peak, all of its riders drunk on a cocktail of fear and excitement and anticipation. I was breathless and unable to stop. I put my foot on the shower wall, bracing myself. My hand worked furiously.

As I got closer, I instinctively held my breath. *No, breathe. Breathe into it and through it.* And so I focused on breathing deeply. The breathing deepened the sensation but lengthened the time it took to climax. I moved closer, then a change of breath inched me away.

Inhale...exhale. Inhale...exhale; nice and smooth. Inhale...

The orgasm caught me on the exhale. I howled as my body clenched and shuddered spasmodically. Wave after wave crashed over me, and I was drowning. My sole thought was to keep my fingers on my clit and my foot on the far wall as my body bucked and jerked.

As the first wave of climax subsided, I pressed down on my clit, feeling its pea-sized stiffness under the folds of my flesh. I came again, nearly as intensely as the last time. This orgasm didn't last quite as long. I rubbed a firm circle around my clit and crumpled again. My abs felt tired. I was spent.

I lay against the far wall of the shower, rubbing my clit every few moments. Each rub was worth a moan and a spasm. I rubbed, ever more gently, until the sounds coming from my body melted into a something between a moan and a hum.

I caught my breath for a moment, then reached for the phone.

I gave the recording a couple of heavy breaths for effect. "I hope you liked that, daddy," I rasped. My voice was deliciously hoarse from the orgasm. I ended the recording, leaned back and spread my legs wide. I took one last photo -- the coup de grace. I'd save that one for another time.

I washed and went to bed.

I took another look at the pictures the next morning, and enjoyed a private smile at the memory of how it felt to take those photos.

After taking the kids to school, I rushed home. I had decided that I'd send the pictures this afternoon.

I looked at the pictures again.

But is it art?

The voice in my head snarked, but I shook my head to erase the thought. I wasn't going to talk myself out of doing this. But I decided to find an artistic-looking filter, to acknowledge the voice. I reasoned that it was a bit less pornographic that way.

I posted the pictures to a private site and sent Julian the link. And then I waited.

It had been a long time since Julian and I last saw each other. I wanted to hear his voice, but I didn't want to feel like I was begging to talk to him. I didn't actually have much to say; I just wanted to go back to our early, flirty conversations. It was true that things had gotten much hotter than in the beginning. They progressed from friendly to flirtatious to heavy with innuendo. And then, Julian sent me my very first dick pic.

I had always thought that I'd be revolted by a dick pic. Instead, I felt an odd mix of emotions; like the guest of honor at a surprise party. It started with shock (*What the.... Did he really just send me this?*), then quickly shifted to a sort of self-effacing pride (*Oh my god. I just got my very first dick pic. I never thought I'd get one of these*). The shock and aw-shucks feelings quickly gave way to amazed enjoyment (*I never thought I'd like something like this, but I can't stop looking at it*), but ended with a bit of a feeling that I don't want this all the time (*I got my first dick pic. I love it. Thanks; I'm good. I don't need more*).

And, of course, there was the fact that it wasn't a dick pic from just anyone, it was from Julian. He was smart enough to have sent it to me after we had slept together many times. I wondered how I would have received it if he'd sent it in the early days of our rekindled relationship. The thought made me laugh, and I nearly choked on my coffee. I already knew the answer. I'd have blocked him and laughed about the whole thing over cocktails with my friends.

But he had gotten the timing and the context right. And he was, of course, him. Before long, he had sent another, and still another. I enjoyed them. I felt a surge of adrenaline every time I saw the message indicator on my phone. It was my naughty secret, and it was perversely satisfying to play this close to getting caught.

And so it felt natural when Julian first asked me to send him pictures. I had expected that he would ask, but I was much more reluctant than he to take nudes. After a few weeks of coaxing from Julian, I sent him my first picture. I had unbuttoned my shirt and taken a picture of my cleavage. I quickly found that I had to adjust the lighting to make myself look good. And I normally took about ten photos for every one that I sent to Julian. He responded with child-like joy. It was very encouraging. I soon graduated to taking more photos, revealing only a little more at a time. I still hadn't sent him a full-body nude. I wasn't ready yet. But I went online to get some tips on taking sexy pictures. If I was going to do it, I wanted to know what I was doing.

The pictures were only part of my pleasure. It felt good to do what Julian asked me to do. I'm not sure how, but I must have signaled that he should take control. He readily took the cue and pushed me until I felt a bit uncomfortable and had to decide to submit or resist. He told me to take a topless selfie in the backyard, and I mildly objected. I'm not that kind of girl, I said. I'm a decent person, I said. But when I sent the picture, I hoped that he would be all the more surprised because of my objections. The truth was that I was exactly that kind of girl, and I enjoyed our little game. He playfully suggested that I call him daddy, and I scoffed. I told him no way, that it's not my thing, while secretly thinking of ways to surprise him with it.

Even so, I felt like I had to engage in this explicit message-trading. If I didn't, I risked losing his attention altogether. I had gotten myself in a mess that I had somehow taken on as a personal challenge. I felt like I was the one who would have to step them down gradually to the place I felt comfortable with. As much as I enjoyed pleasing Julian, I didn't like the idea of sharing my naked pictures.

It wasn't just with him; I had always avoided taking nudes. In my experience, guys just couldn't resist sharing them. There were too many girls in my high school who had made that mistake only to find that they had been betrayed; that their pictures had been shared all around school.

The last thing I wanted was for Julian to get angry and try to blackmail me with them. I cringed to think that I could find myself on one of those revenge porn sites where angry ex-boyfriends, ex-husbands and ex-lovers exacted their revenge by posting explicit pictures and videos.

In truth, both Julian and I had something to lose if we got caught. When I asked him what he had done with the pictures, he told me that he uses them when he takes "alone time," and that they make him feel close to me. Then, he assured me that they were in a safe place where no one could get to them

There wasn't much more that I could do about it.

He never asked what I did with his pictures. For a long time, I had deleted them. I was terrorized by the thought that the girls might stumble on them while playing with my phone. But at some point, I had decided to download and store some of his pictures...just in case. At least I had been careful not to include my face in most of my pictures. Somehow, that made me feel protected. That, and the mutually-assured destruction setup that I had engineered by storing his photos.

Soon, Julian starting sending sexy text messages every day, usually with pictures. It was hard to keep up.

Go ahead, dummy. Keep telling yourself that you're using each other. It's a convenient way to ignore the fact that Julian is using you to get his rocks off.

I don't know at what point it became too much, but I found myself unsure of how to get myself out of the situation. I didn't know how to tell him to stop without making him feel bad. I also didn't know how to get a conversation back on track. Every conversational turn led to a dirty joke or a sexual reference, which led to more pictures. And I wasn't innocent in the situation. Sometimes I just felt sexy and wanted to reel him in to share a little fun time with me. It felt like a trap that I wanted to escape only some of the time.

Six hours and I haven't heard anything. W-T-absolute-F.

My chest clenched as if I was going to hyperventilate. The link worked; I had checked. I just had to wait a bit longer. The only way that he hadn't responded to my message was if he hadn't actually seen the pictures.

It seemed like such a good idea at the time....

Sometimes I hated the voice in my head. Usually, it was like a naughty co-conspirator. Right now, it was working against me; trying to make me lose my nerve. I focused instead on making dinner. I even broke my own rule about making separate meals for each of the girls. I just needed something to occupy me. Tonight, It was macaroni and cheese for Inanna, grilled chicken for Kali, chicken nuggets for Morgan and a hefty side of green beans for them all.

"I thought we had stopped making individual meals for the girls." Aaron stopped mid-stride as he walked past the kitchen with his laptop. He sounded concerned.

"I just don't have the energy to deal with everyone's objections tonight," I sighed. "It's honestly just easier to give in to the terrorists right now."

He looked at me warily, then walked to the table where the girls were eating.

"Girls, when your mother or I cook a meal for you, you can expect to eat it, whether you like it or not. Today's dinner is *not* normal," he warned. "You're very lucky to have a mother who cares enough to make what each of you like to eat. When I was growing up, my brother loved fish, and I don't mean fish sticks. And when my mother cooked fish for dinner, I had to eat it, too."

He was in full-on dad mode. I loved him so much, just like this. Scolding our children in my defense.

The kids didn't care. They munched their food with the benign entitlement of children who have never known anything but love. Besides, they loved every kind of fish we cooked for them. I massaged Aaron's lower back, rubbing it in small circles with the heel of my hand. Aaron turned and bundled me in his arms. I cast a look toward the girls and shrugged. He pursed his lips and shook his head. We craned our necks toward each other and kissed lightly.

* * *

Julian's response came later that night. It was exactly what I had hoped for.

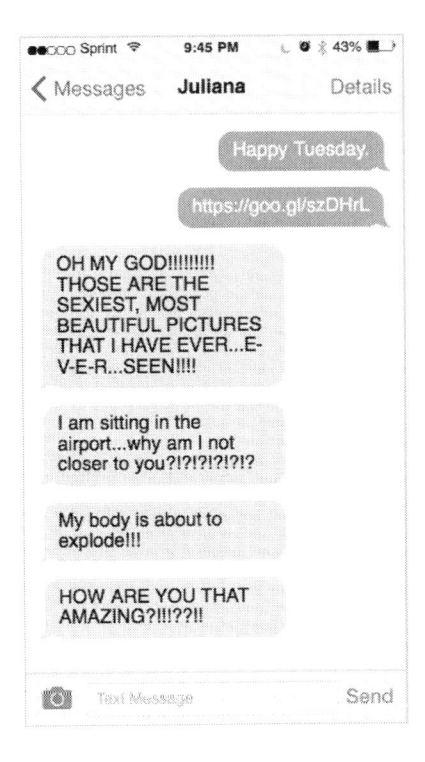

> **Juliana:**
> OH MY GOD!!!!!!!!
> THOSE ARE THE SEXIEST, MOST BEAUTIFUL PICTURES THAT I HAVE EVER...E-V-E-R...SEEN!!!!
>
> I am sitting in the airport...why am I not closer to you?!?!?!?!?!?
>
> My body is about to explode!!!
>
> HOW ARE YOU THAT AMAZING?!!!??!!

The next day's message was even better. I read and re-read both, relishing what felt like power.

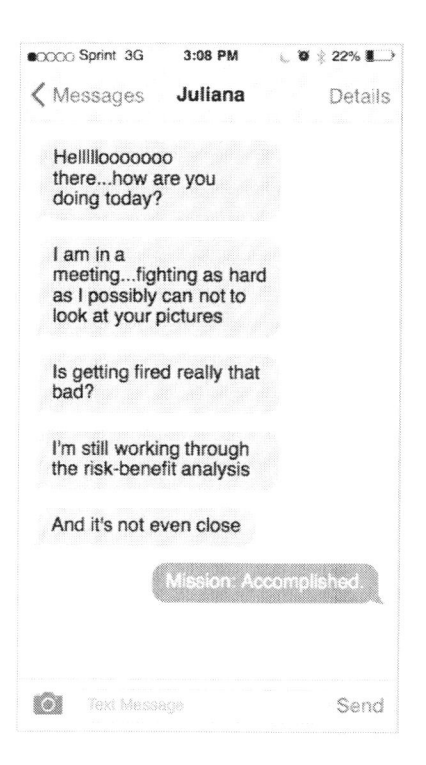

> **Juliana**
>
> Hellllooooooo there...how are you doing today?
>
> I am in a meeting...fighting as hard as I possibly can not to look at your pictures
>
> Is getting fired really that bad?
>
> I'm still working through the risk-benefit analysis
>
> And it's not even close
>
> >> Mission: Accomplished

    I wasn't really some temptress who just wanted to exchange sexy pictures. What I really wanted was to have Julian near me; to hear his voice and smell his skin. I wanted a normal conversation that didn't end with dick pics. But if neglect from Julian was going to be the new normal in this relationship, I had to turn the situation to my advantage. I had to win.

8.1

PUBLIC DISPLAY OF AFFECTION

"THUNDERCATS, HOOOOOOOO!"

Lily and Roland giggled and tucked themselves under a blanket in his dorm room.

"Oh my gosh, I used to watch Thundercats every day after school," she gushed.

"It was my favorite cartoon!" Roland thought for a moment. "Well, that and He-Man."

Lily wrinkled her nose.

"You don't like He-Man?" Roland shook his head dramatically. "Wow. I knew there was something funny about you."

"It was all about She-Ra for me," she replied.

"Okay, okay," he conceded. He swept her hand in both of his and gave it a light kiss.

Roland was a giant of a young man, and his football teammates called him Bear. He was gentle and sweetly romantic, and they had taken their new relationship slowly. Lily had just finished grieving her latest breakup with Julian, and was ready to start dating again when his teammate and best friend Brian caught up with her as she walked across campus one morning.

"You and Julian aren't together anymore, are you?"

Lily was taken aback. "No, we're done. We broke up a while ago."

"Yeah. Like, three weeks ago, right?" Brian pretended be casual about his very specific knowledge of Lily's relationship.

Lily considered the conversation she was having with Brian. It hadn't really occurred to her that she and Julian were one of those couples. Brian wasn't the first guy to ask about her relationship status during her breaks with Julian. It wasn't flattering. It was kind of embarrassing. People were watching. She was part of a long-running, highly passionate and sadly dysfunctional relationship. Julian was as private as she was, and she was pretty sure that he didn't talk about their relationship. Besides, he didn't hang out with the football set. She cringed at the thought that their relationship was infamous, and that people outside of her circle actually tracked her relationship status.

"More or less, I guess."

Lily was intentionally vague. It had actually been three weeks and two days. They had broken up on a Thursday. She had cried until Monday, and had holed herself in her room. She had survived mostly on a stash of crackers, eaten in front of her best friend who demanded proof that Lily was actually eating.

She was eager to put the latest chapter with Julian behind her, so she let Brian introduce her to Roland. One of her few dating rules was that she would only go out with people to approached her directly. But she knew Bear peripherally, and was interested to get to know him better.

They were both music lovers. Lovers of '80s afternoon

cartoons and of dive Mexican food. And as they spent the next few weeks together, the discovered that they genuinely liked each other. They would stay up late watching movies in his dorm room, kissing a little and enjoying the sensation of their still-clothed bodies as they sat close to one another. Roland had admired her from afar during her rocky relationship with Julian, and had written a stash of poems dedicated to her. He revealed them to her sheepishly over the first few weeks of their romance, and finally confessed that he had wanted to be with her since he first saw her. Lily was overwhelmed by his sincerity. His writing was poignant and smart and made her feel honored. It felt like the beginning of something big.

Suddenly, Lily had a new set of adjunct friends. Burly guys who she barely knew suddenly knew her name and would speak to her in passing. These were people who she had seen before, but didn't know and had no reason to speak with. It occurred to her that these must be Roland's teammates. She kind of liked it. There seemed to be friendly faces everywhere.

Lily answered the knock at the door. She was writing an anthropology paper, and was grateful for the distraction. It was probably her hallmate Brie, looking for a similar distraction from her economics paper. Lily took her ponytail down and shook her hair out before looking through the peephole.

"Shit," she whispered. It was Julian. She opened the door.

He stood before her and looked at her meaningfully, using his height to full advantage. He then leaned down and kissed her neck, her hands, her tears. Her body opened to him. She felt herself unfolding, engorging at his kiss. She hated that he made her body respond this way, even when she was upset with him. She was convinced that this was part of the reason why he never said the words "I'm sorry."

They made love in the bed, in the communal shower, and again in her bed that night. He held her aloft by the hips as he thrust into her; took her from behind as she leaned against the shower walls; she took him into her mouth on her knees as the water cascaded over them.

The next day, Julian was ecstatic. As they walked to lunch together, he grasped her hand. Lily paused. They had broken up and gotten back together like this more times than she cared to count. It was so unlike Julian to show any public display of affection, so why was he holding her hand in public now?

Lily worried about how she would tell Roland about their reconciliation. He deserved to know directly from her that she was back with Julian before she let anyone see them holding hands like this. But this was so unusual and so...nice. She decided to relax and enjoy the feeling of being hand in hand in public with him.

Lily never got the chance to let Roland down easily. By that evening, his teammates had closed ranks around him. Bear wasn't home, they said. He couldn't come to the phone, they said. After a few attempts to reach Roland, they answered her persistence with narrowed eyes and pointed silence.

Walking hand-in-hand with Julian killed her budding relationship with Roland. From then on, there were no more warm greetings from the friendly giants around campus.

8.2

HUNGER

I OPENED MY EYES AND STARED AT THE CEILING. Blue pre-dawn light bathed the room. All was silent. I closed my eyes again and listened. Silence. My stomach had stopped complaining late last night after the girls went to bed. That was good. I had made it to Day Three.

It was a progression that I knew well: Day One hunger had started off mad and ended up desperate. As usual, my body had thrown a full-blown tantrum, sending me rummaging wildly through the cabinets and eyeing the kids' snacks lustily; opening and closing the refrigerator and fighting against the force of nature and of habit to put something, anything, in my belly.

Day Two hunger had been predictably earnest. My body had pleaded with me to eat something. I placated it with a small glass of orange juice in the morning and a glass of wine in the evening. The alcohol had given me a nice, heady buzz, but only filed the sharpest edges off of the hunger, which had settled in and refused to go away. It made me dizzy and weak, testy and morose.

It set one part of my mind against the other; the part that knows that I must eat clashing with the part that wanted to punish my body to ease my mind. I had gone to bed that night willing myself to stay under the covers; to fight all thoughts of food; to focus instead on the siren song that lay on the other side of Day Two.

Day Three, as always, would bring sweet euphoria.

An incendiary mix of guilt and heartache and humiliation had roared to a blaze inside of me. It burned and raged, fed by the feeling that I was completely isolated from anything or anyone that could help me. The Hunger, I reasoned, was my controlled burn. I was setting a perimeter to contain and control the pain.

I looked at the clock. I had passed the 72-hour mark as of midnight and was now in The Zone. The Zone was control. All protest was dead. I was light and empty and focused, and felt like I could stay in The Zone forever. All I had to do was make sure the girls didn't notice what I was doing. I sat up in bed, feeling the emptiness in my stomach. It grumbled just a little, but didn't register as hunger. It was only a sound. I swung my feet to the floor, threw on my robe and shuffled to the kitchen to make coffee.

I took a scoop of glossy whole beans and deposited them into the grinder. This was my favorite part. And since I wasn't really eating, the sensuousness of preparing the coffee took on outsized importance. The anticipation brought on an unwelcome flashback. Suddenly, I could smell his skin and hear his breath. Without warning, my body remembered his entry into me. I shuddered. The intensity of the memory surprised me. I was alone in my kitchen, but still felt embarrassed.

We had only talked a handful of times over the last nine months or so, and most of my memories of him had started to fade. Trying to remember was like trying to embrace a ghost. In fact, I struggled to recall some of the most interesting things he had said. I felt badly about this, but couldn't decide why. Maybe it was because my body remembered everything. It was like he had left an imprint on me.

I had committed details of our last encounter to memory: the look on his face as I sat astride him, first finding the right spot and then easing into the rhythm of my strokes; controlling his position with my thighs. I could see his face, brow knitted; eyes glazed with amazement.

Remember his face, I had thought, looking deeply into his eyes while riding him. *Remember this moment*. I noted my hair, in a wild, dark mane around me. I watched him watch me; each move of my hips reflected on his face. I watched him strain against his own climax and finally succumb. I remembered the way he tried to conceal his delight when I told him that I wanted him again and again. I remembered that I throbbed with pain after multiple rounds, but still wanted him. I remember wincing as I slathered coconut oil on my labia, and remarked to myself that my facial moisturizer doubled as a damn fine lube. I remembered milking the very end of his climax, sliding my eyes shut as I moved the tip of his member back and forth over the entrance to my cervix. "Was something different this time?" he had asked. And I remembered how sweetly I had lied, assuring him that nothing was different; everything was just fine. But he was right. I was recording these moments so that I'd have them when we were over.

"Mo-ooom!" Morgan's voice echoed down the hall moments before she appeared behind me in the kitchen. "Mom, Inanna is in my room again. I told her to make her bed and she won't do it."

I closed my eyes and mused that all tattling seems to be done in the same tone of voice. I had just gotten into The Zone and didn't have the energy to deal with kid drama before my cup of coffee.

Inanna appeared, wearing nothing but panties and socks. "No, I didn't! I didn't do that."

"Didn't do what?" I asked, narrowing my eyes for emphasis.

Inanna cast her eyes about, searching as if the answer could be found on the kitchen floor. "I don't know," she replied.

"Didn't get dressed? Didn't make your bed?" I suggested.

Inanna looked down at her naked belly and froze as if she just realized that she was in her underwear. She disappeared. Morgan trailed after her, triumphant.

I poured myself a mug of coffee and inhaled its perfume before taking a sip. It felt lovely going down. I was relieved. Before long, the caffeine would quiet the distant feeling of hunger and I'd be able to function.

I checked my phone again. Still no message from Julian. I am a stupid girl. He had promised to text more often, and I had believed him. And now here I was, checking my phone from the moment I woke up each morning until well past my bedtime, hoping for little more than a hello from him.

Of course he hasn't sent a message. Why would he? He only seems to be interested in my body, anyway.

I had finally told Julian that I wasn't interested in just being a sexting partner, and I was encouraged by his response. He had said that he would make an effort to call more; to text whenever he had a chance. He had said that he didn't want to lose my friendship, and that it meant so much to him to have me in his life again that he would accept any terms that I required. That was three weeks and two days ago. I had sent him a couple of text messages saying hello. It had taken him nine hours to reply to my first message and three days to reply to the second one. I hated myself for having sent that second message. By the beginning of week three, I deleted his name from my contacts. It didn't matter. His phone number was still burned in my brain.

I should have known better. Stupid, stupid girl.

I closed my eyes and pushed my thoughts away, focusing instead on the sensation of emptiness in my belly. I had only had a few sips of coffee; not nearly enough for it to blunt the gnawing feeling. I put my mug down. I wasn't ready to be anesthetized against the pain. Not yet.

I heard the quick slap of naked feet on the hardwood floor. Inanna ran into the room.

"Mom! My Band-Aid came off!" She twisted her outstretched arm to get a look at her elbow.

"That's OK," I reassured her as I searched for the light scratch on her arm

"We put it on last night and your body has healed. You don't need it anymore."

"But I *do* need it," she protested.

I didn't have the energy to push back against a six-year-old's Band-Aid lobbying efforts.

"Let's see how it feels when we have breakfast, OK? If you need me to put another one on, I'll do it."

That answer seemed to satisfy her. She twirled happily, feet squeaking on the floor as she spun.

I was getting annoyed. "Make. Your. Bed. This is the second time I've had to tell you this morning."

Inanna froze, stumbling momentarily as her inner ear adjusted to the sudden stop, then ran out of the room.

"And what made you take your socks off?" I called after her. "We're getting ready for school! Put your socks back on!"

I cradled my coffee in my hands and shuffled to the bedroom. This was promising to be a morning filled with kid drama, and I barely had the energy to deal with it.

I spent the remainder of the morning going through the motions with the girls. Directing a change of clothes for Inanna, making sure that Morgan put on deodorant (she was still inconsistent about using it), locating Kali's English paper after she had mis-labeled and mis-filed it on my computer, packing a snack for Inanna, signing a permission slip for Kali ("Mo-om, this has to be returned today!" "But you're just showing it to me now!") and cooking breakfast for all three of the girls before driving Inanna and Morgan to school. Kali preferred to walk to school than be seen with her own mother. And thank goodness I had a spare Band-Aid floating around in my purse. Halfway through the drive to school, Inanna started howling about needing a new one on her non-existent wound. I stumbled through all of this in a fog, waiting for all of the children to clear the space so that I could have some time alone.

I cleared the girls' plates that they had left on the table in their haste, taking care to avoid sneaking a bite of toast from Kali's plate. I knew that if I ate a corner of toast, I'd go right back to eating normally. I wasn't ready to stop punishing myself yet. Denying myself that single bite felt good; like I had things under control. If I could stay away from a crust of toast, I could avoid sending Julian a text. If I sent him a text, I'd be handing over all control to him. I couldn't let that happen. I preferred to be my own tormentor.

I put the dishes in the dishwasher and wiped down the countertops. All traces of that morning's food were now gone, and the dishwasher hummed and swished in the background. Everything was under control. That was good. I poured myself another cup of coffee, grabbed my laptop from my bedroom and opened a private search window.

I hesitated for a moment. It felt strange to let my fingers type the words. *I am having an affair with a married man.* The first search page returned article after finger-wagging article about sleeping with a married man. Some were cheeky, suggesting that it was a cool, modern thing to do. For a moment, I let myself think that I was making a cool-girl decision. Just as quickly, I let that thought go. This was different.

Other articles rehashed the age-old cautionary tale: man meets woman, man seduces woman, woman falls in love, man freaks out and goes back to wife. I scoffed at those tropes. Those people didn't know what they were talking about. That wasn't my situation at all.

When I stumbled on a couple of chat forums, it felt like I'd finally hit a vein. An anonymous married woman had written to say that she is in love with and is having an affair with a married man. But her husband has a terminal illness. Shoot. That wasn't relevant. Another woman posted about escaping her abusive relationship after meeting and having an affair with a man at work. In both cases, the comments sections brimmed with responses. People either condemned the women ("Keep it up; you're a great example for your kids!") or sympathized with the tragedy of their marriages. There seemed to be no sympathy for women who have affairs. Then again, was I really expecting people to feel sympathetic? The only outcome of an affair is pain.

I closed the browser window and pressed my fingers to my temples. My head ached. As I tried to quiet my throbbing head, my stomach seemed to double over onto itself with hunger. The hunger pain was good. The headache was bad. I put on water for tea. Maybe I could hydrate my way out of this headache.

I remembered how it felt when I found out that my own father had had an affair with another woman. That was when I realized that my family was vulnerable; that there was no such thing as a safe place. What was my problem? Why was I doing this to my own family? Everyone says that there must be a reason. The women on the forums were dealing with illness or abuse or total lack of attention from their husbands. The closest I could come to a reason was boredom. Loneliness. Maybe I missed the woman I used to be. But who didn't?

My water was boiling now. I grabbed a tea bag and a teapot, and poured the water over the tea bag. I hated feeling guilty. I had to stop the feeling. I thought about screwing Julian in the bathroom at the secret restaurant. That had made me feel dangerous, sexy, alive. I thought about the look on his face when I unzipped his pants and begged to take him into my mouth. I savored that memory for a moment. It had been too long since I'd heard from him.

I poured some tea into a mug, inhaled the sharp spearmint aroma and took a sip. The too-hot tea burned the tip of my tongue. I winced, cursing myself for drinking too soon.

Shoot! that spot on my tongue will feel dead for the next day.

I rubbed my injured tongue against the roof of my mouth, then laughed aloud at the irony. It was that little bit of death that reminded me that I'm alive.

* * *

Kali and I sat across from each other in a booth next an oversized, sunny window. Our shopping bags were crowded in a pile next to me -- our haul from a very special afternoon of shopping. Kali's 16th birthday was coming up soon, and just as my great-aunt had done for me at that age, I had taken her shopping for her first real lingerie.

"Happy Birthday, Kali. You're an amazing girl. I'm so incredibly proud of you."

"Thanks, mom," she mumbled into her food. "I just wish I weren't so..." she trailed off.

"Wish you weren't so...what?"

"So...you know, chubby."

I exhaled, pressed my fingertips together and brought them to my lips. It was impossible to tell her how perfect she was. I had been a sixteen-year-old girl before, and there was certainly nothing that anyone could have said to convince me that I was as lovely as I actually was.

"You know you're getting old when you start saying things like 'When I was your age...,' but here goes."

I cleared my throat for emphasis.

"When I was your age, I couldn't see how beautiful I was, either. It didn't matter what anyone said. As for feeling chubby, I started thinking I was fat when I was in second grade."

"Really?" Kali stared, wide-eyed. "I didn't start thinking I was fat until fourth grade."

I winced, but tried to recover before it registered with Kali.

"The thing is, you really are that incredible. Everything about you right now is exactly how it's supposed to be, including the voice in your head that makes you doubt yourself sometimes. The world can see how beautiful you are. It's all part of a cruel maturational joke that you're the only one who can't see it."

She looked at me, bemused.

"It happens to all of us. Trust me, by the time you hit your 20's, you'll be magnificent. At that point, you'll know it, too. What an amazing time. That'll last for 10 or 20 years, depending on lots of things. Then, at some point, it'll all go to hell."

I hoped that my prediction would make her laugh. I had made it easy for her. After all, I was the butt of the joke.

"So, when does that happen?" Kali asked wickedly. She had picked up on my lead.

"Hmmm...how old am I? 42? Then it starts to happen at around age 43," I answered with mock authority. "Definitely 43. But I'm not going out without a fight." I grinned.

"Is that why you aren't eating?"

My face fell. I felt the blood drain from my cheeks. The gnawing hunger in my belly fell away, leaving a pit of shame. I should have known better. I couldn't hide anything from my children. They studied my every move.

"No," I replied softly. I took a deep breath, studying my plate. "I've been feeling kind of anxious...well, very anxious, about some things lately."

I looked at Kali and saw concern in her eyes.

"It's nothing for you to worry about," I said, reaching

across the table to grasp her hand. "I need to be more aware..."

I was starting to lie, but decided to stop.

"I need to make some better decisions about how I handle it. Clearly, not eating is not the way to go."

I squeezed Kali's hand and gave a tight grin. I was desperate to change the subject.

"You know, you noticed that and pointed it out. It wasn't easy to do that, I'm sure." I nodded reassuringly. "You're an amazing girl. I love you so much, it's impossible for you to understand. It's like my love is a bubble all around you. A love bubble."

Kali was starting to look embarrassed. She freed her hand from mine.

"I don't care if you don't want to hold my hand," I teased. "I still love you. You could be a serial killer and I'd still love you."

"Mom, *stop*."

I continued, in a high-pitched, mock-maternal tone.

"That's my baby, the serial killer. Isn't she wonderful? And look at those eyes. Wait, don't look in her eyes. That's how she gets you. But that's my baby."

"Oh my god, mom," she said, laughing a little in spite of herself.

"Oh, thank you, sweetheart. You just made my day. You know, it just isn't complete without a good, 'Oh my god, mom.' Thank you. I'll sleep well tonight."

We sat, looking at each other for a few moments. Kali was my first child. I wanted everything wonderful that the world has to offer to rain down at her feet. At the same time, I knew that wouldn't happen; that so much had already happened in her world that I would never know about. But still, here she was, as perfect as ever. Every bump in the road that she had encountered; every scar that she would bear from a life well-lived would only make her more so. My heart swelled until it felt like it might burst out of my chest.

"What is it?" she asked.

"You remember my aunt TT, right?" TT was actually my great-aunt, but was like one of my closest girlfriends when I was growing up.

"I remember," Kali nodded. "She owned a bunch of businesses and traveled all over the world, then sold them for a bunch of money. She was a badass."

"Hey," I objected. "You're getting kind of sassy with the language, aren't you?"

Kali gave me a look.

"Well, yes. She was a badass."

We both giggled a bit. It felt so good to be giggling with my teenage daughter. I wished that I could crystallize this moment.

"Right." My voice dropped to a conspiratorial tone. "Well, there are a few stories about her that I *haven't* told you. I think you're old enough to hear about them now."

Kali leaned in with a hungry look. "Tell me." Her eyebrows waggled.

"TT was the one who bought me my first underwear that wasn't white and cotton." I smiled at the memory. "I was sixteen, just like you. I remember it was this little green lace number. It reminded me a little bit of this..."

I reached into the bag as if I were planning to expose Kali's new lingerie purchase.

"Don't you dare," she spat.

"Relax, I'm just kidding." I pulled my hand out of the bag. "But seriously, I think she was, like, 72 at the time. Smoked like a chimney."

Kali wrinkled her nose at the thought of my chain-smoking great-aunt. I waved the gesture away.

"Yeah, she was 72 and I was 16 -- I remember because she took me out for my birthday and bought me this amazing lingerie. We were sitting on the terrace at a restaurant downtown with her hair blowing in the wind and cigarette smoke blowing all around. She had three boyfriends at the time. Told me all about them."

Kali nearly choked on her food. "My great-great aunt had three boyfriends? At one time? At 72 years old?"

"Yup," I confirmed. "And one of them was a plumber. She was very clear about how important it is to have a good plumber in your life." I gave a her a wink for emphasis.

Kali's eyes searched the ceiling as if she'd find an answer there.

"Oh...my...you're talking about TT? Sweet little TT?" Kali's memories of my great-aunt were of a 96-year-old woman. It was hard for her to imagine TT as the force that she once had been.

I continued. "Anyway, she told me this crazy story about her time with Harry Belafonte, but that's a story for another day. The point is that he called her a dangerous woman."

Kali looked at me blankly.

I pulled out my phone and googled pictures of a young Harry Belafonte.

"Ohhhh," she replied.

"I know," I concurred. We swiped through a few more pictures. "The point is," I said, placing my phone on the table, "that

TT was incredible. It wasn't just that she was a great businesswoman. She started with nothing. She left home when she was just seventeen and was out in the world on her own."

"She was a model," Kali sighed, resting her elbows on the table and her chin in her upturned palm.

"No career is as glamorous as it seems, especially that one," I lectured. "She was a child, out in the world on her own. And the world can be an unforgiving place that eats beautiful girls for breakfast and poops them out before lunch." I nodded toward her meaningfully. "But TT managed to get out there and survive. More than that, she lived. She really lived. The fact that a man like that --" I pointed at the face of a young Harry Belafonte smiling seductively on my phone screen "called her a dangerous woman is part of the proof."

"Okay, I get what you're saying," Kali said, removing her elbows from the table and placing her hands in her lap. "Just...could you...I mean..."

"Just say it, sweetheart."

"Could you stop buying me so many condoms? I'm running out of places to put them!" She whisper-yelled at me, leaning across the table for emphasis.

"Well, how am I supposed to know that you're good on condoms unless you tell me?" I whispered back. "Besides, I buy them at Costco. You can't beat the price."

"It's official. I have the craziest mother ever," Kali declared. She rolled her eyes and shook her head.

"Come on. I'm not *the* craziest mother ever."

She looked back at me. One corner of her mouth curved into a smirk.

"Listen, I want you to know that I'm here for you when

you're ready to talk about this stuff. People have been having sex since the beginning of...of people, I guess. And yes, even women like your sweet old great-aunt have had plenty of it. Nothing about it is new. When you need me, I am absolutely here for you." I reached my hand across the table and made a slight beckoning movement with my fingers. She didn't take my hand.

"Mom, I'm not having sex."

"Oh, thank God."

"But thank you for being there for me." Her tone was sheepish, sincere.

"Absolutely. I'm here whenever you need me."

She reached out, and I took her hand in mine. I brought it to my lips and kissed the back of her fingers, then gave her hand a little squeeze.

* * *

"It's really good to talk to you on the phone. I feel like we've been texting each other a lot lately." I silently cursed myself for not saying what I really meant.

"It's good to talk to you, too." Julian's voice was playful. "But I'd love to hear you do a little more than just talk. You sound so good when you're...excited."

"Well, that's the thing. We haven't talked -- or even texted -- in a really long time. I just want to talk to you."

"I want to talk to you, too." His voice was still playful.

I sighed. I was going to have to be very clear with him. "Seriously. I have a little more going on than just sex."

Julian paused.

"You're right. I'm sorry. I never should have presumed that's what you wanted."

I was relieved, but also a bit alarmed. That apology came a little too easily. I wondered why.

"I'll do my best to behave."

I didn't want him to feel chastised. After all, I was a very willing participant. "I want to be clear: sex with you is amazing. And I love seeing you. You are absolutely magnificent."

"Don't worry about it; I get it. It's just that when I see pictures of you, I feel closer to you. I want to see you all the time." His tone changed. "Remember the first time we got together? In New York?"

"Of course."

"That was the first time I had had sex in six months."

It wasn't the first time he had said something about having a sexless marriage. I had wondered what he meant when he first told me, but somehow it seemed wrong to ask. One of our unwritten rules was that we didn't ask probing questions about our spouses. I wondered if that was true. Maybe it didn't matter. Even if he were lying, would I have done anything differently? Probably not.

"Oh," I answered. I tried not to sound too interested, too surprised or too judgemental. I gave myself a mental pat on the back for striking exactly the tone I had been going for.

"For me -- well, for a lot of men -- sex is about intimacy."

"I should hope so."

"Okay, maybe I didn't explain myself very well. The urge to be with your woman is as strong an urge as hunger," he explained. "I know that men and women experience intimacy differently, but don't you think it's fair that if a man spends time listening to his woman talk through her problems that she should spend time with him when he needs intimacy?"

"Those don't seem like equivalent needs to me," I replied.

He went on as if he didn't hear me. "And you and I have done a lot of talking. I just really want to be with you. And if I can't be with you, I want to see pictures of you."

"Okay, let's go back to your point about the kind of intimacy that men and women need. Here's the way I see it." I took a breath and spoke slowly. "Let's say, for example, that you have a neighbor who you like very much, and who likes to come over and visit. You enjoy having this neighbor over, and you like their company very much. But sometimes, you just want them to stay in their own damned house. Why do they have to come over every single day? Don't they have their own house? Because every time they come over, you have to be ready to entertain, and then clean up afterward. Sometimes you want to talk to them but don't want to do all that. At times like that, it sure would be nice to talk on the phone."

"You're going to have to explain that one," he said, deadpan. "I have no idea what you're talking about."

"I'm a woman. My body is like my house. I enjoy everything about you and like spending time with you. But you can't come over every day. There. I said it."

Julian laughed. I giggled a little, too.

"And don't just send me pictures of your house when you're feeling friendly. Pick up the phone sometimes."

"Okay, I get it," he laughed. His tone changed suddenly. "But seriously, sex makes me feel loved and attractive. It's what keeps me motivated to continue to get up and kill myself at work every day."

"Don't you think that puts your wife in a position where she feels like she has to provide sex in exchange for the basics? I hate break it to you, but that makes sex a chore, not a pleasure."

"That's fine!" he was excited. "The whole thing is transactional, anyway." He sounded triumphant, as if he'd made his ultimate point. It occurred to me that he and my friend Kelly would make a fine match. They were both fine with transactional sex in a relationship.

"Is that so?" I paused to emphasize the point. "Then, what exactly do you think I'm getting out of this relationship?"

"I don't like where this is going," he scoffed. "You're starting to sound like my wife."

* * *

"So, I hear that a man's need for sex can be compared to a feeling like hunger."

Aaron stopped swiping the screen on his phone, thinking, his thumb still in mid-air. "Yeah, I think that's a decent analogy."

"Well, I've also heard people say that if a husband is expected to listen attentively to his wife that she, in turn, should provide him with sex whenever he wants it."

He gave me a strange look. "As much as I like that idea, I just don't think it's true. I'd say that if a husband is expected to listen to his wife that she should extend him the same courtesy."

"And that's why you're the man for me." I threw my arms around his neck and kissed his cheek. "You know, the problem I have with the hunger analogy is this: If a man's sexual need is like hunger, which I get, asking his wife for sex is not analogous asking her to prepare a meal for him."

"Okay...." Aaron put his phone down.

I got excited. I was feeling clever. "Instead, it's like asking her to eat with him. She may or may not be hungry. She may not want to eat what he wants to eat. Because maybe he wants to eat the same thing every time. Or maybe there's something he wants to eat that she thinks is completely disgusting. Or..."

Aaron's eyes had glazed over and he was looking at me with a silly grin.

"What?" I asked suspiciously.

"Well, you know in those old cartoons when one of the characters is just starving?"

"Yes?"

"And he looks over at his buddy, who's usually just chatting away?"

"Yeah..."

"And he hallucinates that his buddy looks just like a nice, juicy, piping hot roast turkey?"

"Oh my god..."

"You look good, girl. Why don't you let me have a taste?"

"You are so silly."

"What? You're the one who started all this talk about men and hunger and sex. And I am just a man."

I wriggled out of his grasp.

*　*　*

It was 3am and I couldn't sleep. I felt like I'd been awake for hours, trying without success to quiet my mind. I missed Julian so much that it hurt. I missed sex with him. I wanted to punish him for making me feel this way. I felt resentful. Angry, even. I wanted him to pay attention to me.

The recording!

The thought hit me out of nowhere. I hopped out of bed, grabbed my earbuds, and opened the voice recording app. I listened to the recording of me pleasuring myself in the shower. It was so fucking hot.

He is going to lose his mind.

Without a second thought, I attached it to a text message.

Well, if you're going to send that recording, you might as well go all in. Now's the time for the coup de grace. Send it, too!

In a few more keystrokes, I had attached the picture of me touching myself. Fingers shaking, I typed, "I'm not one for mixed messages, but I can't help how much I want you. Sweet dreams." I took a deep breath, held it, closed my eyes and hit send.

That's it. I think I just broke text messaging. If I never hear from him again, at least I know I went out like a boss.

I felt wild and amazing. And part of me wanted to knock him on his backside with my message. I knew that the recording would delight him, but what I really hoped was that the picture would give him the surprise of his life. I certainly never expected a single one of the many dick pics he had sent me over the last several months.

Let's see how he handles the twat shot that I just sent.

With that, I powered my phone off, swaggered downstairs to the kitchen and pulled out a Tupperware container with leftover macaroni and cheese from a couple of nights ago. I cut a wedge of it with the edge of a soup spoon and put it on a pretty gold-edged porcelain salad plate. I added truffle oil and cayenne pepper. Just before I slid into my seat, I remembered: Macaroni and cheese is so much better with a little whiskey. I danced to the liquor cabinet and poured a little of my favorite rye whiskey, neat, into a lowball glass. Then I poured a little more for good measure, giggling at my own devilry. I sat down and ate the sexed-up macaroni and cheese cold, alternating spoonfuls of it with sips of whiskey. It was divine.

9.1

A DANGEROUS WOMAN

IT HAD BEEN LONG DAY WITH CLIENTS. SHE HAD spent the day had introducing her team to their client counterparts, making sure that her clients could and put a face -- and personality -- to the names that they knew so well already.

There was Jason, the business school graduate whose arrogance was only made tolerable by his charm. And he was indeed charming. He had large, watery dark brown eyes fringed with the kind of lashes that Lily had paid many hundreds of dollars to mimic. He had a knack for connecting with people, and easily made himself the center of attention in social situations. Naturally, he was the life of every party. His sense of humor was impish; sometimes bawdy, but never vulgar. It was a fine line that was hard not to appreciate. But no matter how you felt about Jason's jokes, when he laughed his big, open-mouthed laugh, it was impossible not to join in.

There was Darius with the meticulously-maintained, jet black locs that nearly reached his waist. He normally pulled them into a neat low chignon for the office, and liked to accessorize with an oversized watch and a pair of horn-rimmed glasses that I wasn't sure he really needed. Put together with his crisp shirt, slacks and tie, Darius could have been a model. His physique was sculpted by football: "I played in high school, but I wasn't good enough for college," he'd demur. None of it mattered. His look was perfect. He'd been out of business school for a while, and had acquired a range of experience from manufacturing to politics. He had an athlete's ease and the real-world chops that come with experience.

Valentina was a fireball, and Lily liked her most of all. It had been a little difficult getting to know her, in part because Valentina had such a hard-nosed personality. In fact, Lily's boss had made Valentina report to her only a few months earlier. The move was probably meant to get the two women to take each other out after Valentina had had a rough encounter with the inexperienced boss. "You'll have to be careful," he had confided, looking sidewise and leaning in close to her. They were alone in his office with the door closed. "Valentina is a dangerous woman." Lily had looked at him for a moment to make sure he wasn't kidding. He was entirely serious.

The truth was that Valentina was only dangerous in that she scared the pants off of the boss. She was whip smart and insanely creative with a nose for bullshit that never failed her. Plus, she had a work ethic like that of the devil himself. The boss had tried to maneuver around her, and she promptly outmaneuvered him, gaining style points for humiliating him in front of the CEO. Moving Valentina onto Lily's team was the latest in the game of chess that was happening between Valentina and the boss. It was his attempt to humiliate her right back. After all, Valentina was two levels more senior than Lily.

It mattered little to Lily. She had decided early on that she liked Valentina. They had laughed over whiskey at the "dangerous woman" comment. Poor little boss. He had no idea how dangerous either of them could be.

"Don't worry about the stupid reporting structure," Lily had promised. "We'll just keep working together the way we always have. Actually, I'm glad to be working more closely with you." She straightened in her club chair and raised her glass.

"To dangerous women," she proposed.

Valentina gave a throaty laugh and raised her glass in answer: "May we always work together."

Brandi had just graduated from college and was eager to learn everything. She reminded Lily of herself at that age, but was much more eager about her job. Brandi knew that she wanted a career in public relations, and wasn't shy about asking Lily for help reaching the top as soon as she could. She worked long and hard, and volunteered to take on extra assignments whenever they were available. She had even moved from her midtown loft to to the rural-based company's headquarters for the better part of a year so that she could be the team's on-site eyes and ears. She was eminently promotable, Lily had judged. She just needed to be maneuvered through a few more experiences to close the deal. Brandi was adorable. She was petite with a button nose and a wide, dazzling grin that she readily shared with just about anyone. Hers was the kind of countenance that inspired good behavior on the hopes that she would grant you the warmth of her smile. This evening, her hair fell in soft waves to just below her chin. She normally wore it in a sleek bun, but had worn it down to meet clients today. The look was soft and pretty, and a big change from her usual look. It was kind of hard to stop looking at her.

And then there was Lily. Her allure was serpentine, seductive. She could start, pivot, or leave a conversation to wither and die with little more than an arched eyebrow. Her smile was a bit less open; more of a smirk. It wasn't really intentional, but it was hers. She had been counseled early on to make clients believe that she's cooler than they are -- a little influencer trick. But that part was easy. She loved talking about music and literature and art and fashion. She had curated a look based on up-and-coming designers with the highest-quality fabrics that she could afford. She believed that a sign of being well-dressed is that people notice the woman first, and then the clothes. She wore dresses that accentuated her silhouette. With breasts and hips like hers, trying to disguise her physique would only backfire, making her look 15 pounds heavier. Julian had once compared her to Jessica Rabbit, which she found laughable -- he always exaggerated to make his point. But from time to time, she'd admire herself in the mirror and purr, "I'm not bad, I'm just drawn that way." Playing gorgeous was great fun.

The bar was packed with the after-work crowd. Darius had spotted an oversized banquette with a low-slung table between the two booths. He nabbed it before anyone else could. The team slid in, grateful to have found room for all four of them. Lily set the tone by ordering a Manhattan and a few appetizers for the table. The rest of the team tucked in with their cocktail orders and commiserated on their day.

Lily spotted him at the bar. It was Peter, one of her most senior clients. He had come in alone. They had run into each other earlier in the day in the hallway. He had greeted her coolly, professionally. Peter was a little stiff whenever she encountered him in the office, but that was excusable, she thought. He was the number two guy in the number one region for one of the largest companies in the world. So, he was a little formal. No big deal.

Lily and Valentina had pitched a proposal to Peter a few months before and had been surprised and excited that he was so generous with his time. Valentina had tried pitching a second, bigger project to him more recently. She had called Lily, breathless with excitement after finishing a call with him.

"Good news!"

"What is -- ?" Lily asked.

Valentina didn't wait for the question. "Peter Reardon wants to have a second meeting about the conference proposal."

"That's fantastic. The idea is solid. Plus, it's impossible to say no to you when you're in full-on pitch mode."

Lily smiled, in part because Valentina was the most persistent person she knew. Of course she had made the sale. She also laughed internally at the way Valentina always called her prospects by their first and last names. Any other person would have just called him Peter.

"I know. There is so much work to do between now and the 20th. He wants to meet us for dinner the night before, then we'll pitch to his entire team the next morning."

"Wait -- us?" Lily hesitated. It wasn't unusual for her to attend this type of meeting, but at this point, this was solidly Valentina's project.

"Yeah. He wanted to make sure you can make it." Valentina spoke slowly.

"He won't do the meeting without you there." There was a bit of a lilt in her voice. They both knew why.

Peter was, apparently, a master of self-restraint when in meetings. But he had made it plain to both of them that he wanted to sleep with Lily.

* * *

He turned in time to catch Lily looking at him from across the room. She waved Peter over, inviting him to join the group. This was a great chance to spend a little time with him informally, and wouldn't put her in a compromising position. It wouldn't be just the two of them -- there were four other people there. I'm a master at rebuffing advances. Should be a piece of cake. She and Valentina exchanged a look. A shadow crossed Valentina's face.

Peter walked over and positioned himself at the head of the table.

"Mind if I join you?" he asked, pulling up a chair from an empty table behind him.

Of course they didn't mind. This was a golden opportunity with one of the team's most senior clients. He held the keys to a bigger scope of work, as long as the team impressed him on the newly-pitched project. And that wouldn't be a problem. This was an excellent team.

Everyone made accommodating noises, trying hard not to sound as if this was the best thing that had happened to them all day. They had spent most of the day jockeying for client attention in the not-so-subtle way that all agencies did. They weren't the only ones in town for the marketing all-team meeting, and Lily wasn't the only one who was there to show off her team. The agencies were supposed to work together, but all of them knew that this was a zero-sum game for budget. Gain favor with a client, and that client might pull funds from another agency to fund your work.

That project could lead to more work and a sweet bonus. The situation was ripe for agencies to backstab each other and clients to press their advantage.

Peter settled into his seat and smiled, confident in his power to bestow favor. After a round of introductions, he chatted easily with Jason and Darius. It turned out that the three of them were in the same fraternity. It was a lucky point of connection. He was more than 20 years their senior and clearly loved being transported back to his youth. They laid it on just enough; gently flattering him while still making him feel like one of them. It was masterful.

By the time the appetizers arrived, Lily was feeling slightly miffed. Peter was so wrapped up in his conversation with the guys that he had hardly spoken to her at all. He had been polite to everyone at the table and had even talked with Valentina a bit about her project. That was good -- they had moved the ball forward a bit -- but, still. It was like she was being iced out.

"Excuse me. I'll just be a moment."

She stood and side-shuffled past Brandi, who was seated next to her. Peter had just said something, and Jason was giving him his big-mouthed laugh. Lily tried not to roll her eyes. She made her way toward the kitchen, hoping to find the ladies' room.

Once inside, she leaned in close to the bathroom mirror. Her lashes normally cast a shadow over her eye color, but now she was so close to the mirror that she could see their cocoa brown ringed with black.

"No, we don't love it, but this is the job," she murmured in response to the thought in her mind.

The woman washing her hands a couple of basins down looked up, startled to see that Lily was talking to herself. Lily caught the woman's look in the mirror and realized that she had been speaking out loud. Didn't matter. She went back to her pep talk.

"Get out there. Get that money." Her eyes flashed.

She returned to the table to find Peter seated on the banquette next to her empty spot.

"I kept it warm for you," he said, inviting her to sit down.

There was nowhere else to sit. Apparently, he had shooed Darius into his seat at the head of the table. Darius shrugged a sort of apology at Lily as she slid into the banquette.

"I came over here because I thought you'd want to spend a bit more time with me," Peter said.

He was leaning in close, his face close to hers. She could feel the warmth of his breath as he spoke. He was sitting next to her and was turned to nearly face her. She mirrored his position.

Instantly, Lily evaluated him. Nope, he wasn't drunk. He had told her before that he didn't drink, and, true to form, had ordered a Coke when he joined them at their table. Peter, the big-deal senior executive, was playing a little dominance game with her. It was pointless to protest that she was a married woman. Her wedding band might as well have been invisible. She decided that she would not be chased away.

"Yes, I do." Lily replied. "I'm so glad that you joined us. It's almost as if you like the work we do."

It was a clever dodge. She cast a quick glance around the table at her team to pull them in. They were all watching.

"Almost," he said.

He held her gaze for a second, then let his eyes wander slowly, openly, down her body. Lily took a deep breath, and relaxed her upper back. She refused to appear nervous. When his gaze met hers again, she was looking at him steadily, eyes narrowed.

His gaze shifted over her shoulder. "She'll have a gin martini." Lily hadn't noticed that the server had appeared. Peter grinned at her. "Dirty, right?"

"Not that kind of girl," Lily replied. She turned around to face the server. "Actually, I'll take a ginger ale, please."

He knew that she was pregnant. She was five months along and her figure-accentuating dress put her baby bump front and center. And surely he had gotten a good look at it when he took that extra-long look at her body a moment before. No matter. There was little point contradicting him. She was sure that he had been just itching to make a dirty martini reference.

The waitress nodded, took more drink orders and offered to bring more appetizers for the table. Peter took the opportunity to order a few more food items. Lily was grateful for the break. Her eyes briefly met Darius' at the head of the table. He gave her a concerned look.

Peter was back at it. "You look really good today. Really good." He cast an approving look at her legs. "You know, when I saw you in that skirt today, I almost --"

"Hey," Lily interrupted brightly. "You said that you graduated U of C in '72, right? My dad was there in '72...no, wait; he graduated in '73." Peter looked mildly stunned, which was exactly the response she had hoped for. "Kenneth Chapman is his name. Any chance that you might know him?"

Something in Peter's eyes changed. He waved off the diversion.

"What daddy doesn't know can't hurt him."

Lily's cheeks felt warm. This guy was focused. It wasn't

going to be easy to wriggle her way out of this conversation. She took a sip of water. As she looked up from her glass, Jason caught her eye.

"Are you okay?" he mouthed.

She gave a single, sharp nod.

Peter was back at it.

"So how about you and me? You should come down to Miami. I could really take care of you." He had leaned in close again.

Lily managed a convincing laugh, as if he had just said something clever.

"Oh, Peter," she smiled at him prettily against everything inside her. "I don't shit where I eat." She batted her eyes at him a couple of times for effect.

That one normally worked to halt any workplace come-ons that Lily encountered. It wasn't an outright rejection, and also served to remind the recipient that dating at work is a bad idea. It was an easy way for both of them to save face while leaving open the possibility of working together in the future.

This time, however, Lily felt like she had been closed in a box whose sides were now crumpling in on her. She was trying to keep composed. Her discomfort wasn't really about the innuendo. This motherfucker is trying to undermine me in front of my team, she seethed.

"You know, you could just find some girl to sleep with who doesn't have a professional services contract with you. Unless you're just into paying for it."

She winced at that last bit. That was a bit too sharp-tongued for a client who held the purse strings. She tried to soften the blow.

"Of course, you don't need to. You're kind of a big deal."

She could see out of the corner of her eye that conversation between Jason, Valentina, Darius and Brandi had stopped. Brandi's mouth was hanging open. Darius' eyes were comically wide. Jason intervened with his social magic.

"So, um, Peter? Darius and I were just talking about our old Lambda days and wanted to know -- hey, do you remember the Devil's Eyes?" He nudged Darius, who quickly snapped out of his shock.

"Yeah, dog. But our chapter stopped all that after my line crossed." Peter's eyes were locked on mine. He was still looking at me as he started his answer. "Yeah, I remember. We used to..."

She gave a silent thanks for her team. They had given her a moment to recover. It was exhausting to spar with Peter, relying entirely on defensive moves and avoiding landing any blows. Plus, he was relentless.

It was clear that Peter wasn't going away anytime soon, so Lily decided to shake him once and for all. She'd take the team back to the hotel bar so that they could unwind and commiserate before tomorrow's meetings. She deftly wrapped up the conversation and announced that they were headed back to the hotel. She had paid the bill and was walking with the rest of the team to the parking lot. Her team had arrived in two cars. Peter, thankfully, peeled off from them to go to his own car.

The team crowded around her as they walked across the parking lot.

"Girl, Peter Reardon was looking at you like he wanted to devour you."

Valentina's voice mingled concern with gossipy delight.

She had been sitting too far away to hear the really sordid parts of the conversation, but Peter's body language had said it all.

"When you got up to go to the ladies' room, he was looking at your body like he could see right through your clothes."

Lily sighed.

"We are so sorry," said Jason. "That behavior does not represent us or our frat at all."

"Yo, I have never seen anything like that," Darius mused, shaking his head in disbelief. "That was so disrespectful. He had no right to push up on you like that. Are you sure you're OK?"

"Guys, I really appreciate your concern. It means a lot to me," Lily replied. She was genuinely grateful to them. "I'm fine. I'm just glad that we got out of there. It's definitely hard to keep him at arm's length."

Darius and Jason exchanged a look.

"Um, Lily..." Darius hesitated. "Peter said that he's going to join us at the hotel."

"Shit," she said in a forceful whisper. "He's actually going to follow me to my hotel."

"Look, you stay in your room. We'll keep him busy until he realizes that you're not coming down. Shouldn't be longer than, what, 15 minutes? 20?" Jason shrugged and looked to Darius and Valentina for validation. They nodded in agreement. Brandi looked on, wide-eyed. She had never been this silent in the entire time Lily had known her.

"We'll text you when he leaves," Valentina promised.

It sounded like a good plan to her. "Perfect," Lily said, nodding.

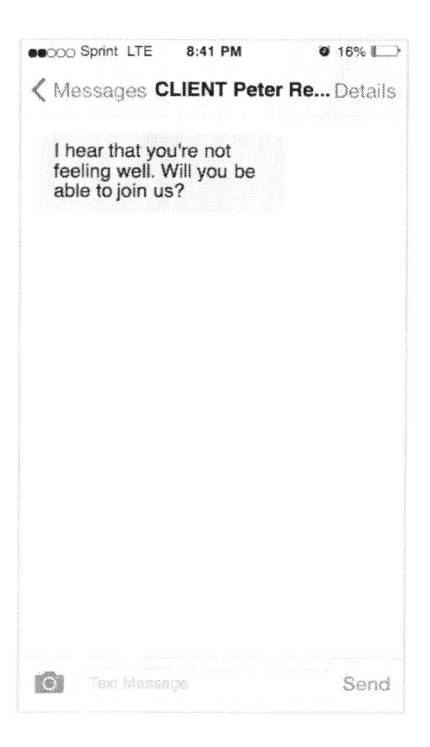

> **CLIENT Peter Re...**
>
> I hear that you're not feeling well. Will you be able to join us?

    He was good at this game. Peter certainly knew better than to leave written evidence of his advances. The chief marketing officer of his company had just been fired a few months before for sleeping with an ad agency leader. It had caused an uproar, and was covered in the national news and gossip rags alike. Lily was amazed that he insisted on trying to bed her under the circumstances. He was bold, and she had witnesses.

    But he was also smart. He had gambled -- correctly -- that Lily wasn't willing to burn down her career just to expose him. Lily hated that he had gotten that right about her.

    She also hated lying to him. It had less to do with a moral conviction than with being in a position of strength. If she were in a better position, she would have told Peter to go directly to hell. Instead, she was holed up in her hotel room like prey, entirely dependent on her team for communication. Fuck Peter.

Still, she couldn't flex too hard against his wishes. He controlled a large budget, and the opportunity for Lily to win a decent chunk of it. For just a moment, she thought about sleeping with him. Didn't some people do it that way? No, that wouldn't work. He'd always hold their secret over her head, and any benefit from their relationship would go to her agency, anyway.

She'd have to reject him without killing the potential for more money. She sat on the corner of the bed and typed out a message.

> **Sprint LTE 8:47 PM 15%**
>
> ‹ Messages **CLIENT Peter Re...** Details
>
> I hear that you're not feeling well. Will you be able to join us?
>
> Thanks for checking in. I have a crushing headache. Trying to relax for a little while before heading downstairs. I'll give it a few more minutes, then I'll join.
>
> Text Message   Send

It couldn't be a normal headache; it had to be a crushing one. And she had to sound like she was gamely trying to collect herself so that she could be available for his advances.

"After all, nothing turns a girl on more than a client who is proposing that you trade sex for money," she said aloud. She rose sharply and walked to the bathroom mirror. "And nothing tells your team that you're a strong leader like sleeping with a client."

She gazed at her reflection. The corners of her mouth twitched with disgust.

She waited for a few minutes, checking her screen periodically. There was no reply from Peter. That was good. She walked back to the bed and flopped backward, arms outstretched.

She would wait at least ten minutes before sending another text.

She suddenly raised her phone in front of her nose. She was typing so fast that she had to re-type her message twice. She messaged Darius and Valentina. There was no use texting Jason, who had already had too much to drink before they had made it back to the hotel. Lily was desperate to know if Peter was still there. Maybe he had gotten bored and moved on. Why would he bother hanging out to wait for her? She had clearly brushed him off, right?

There was no answer from either of them. Damn. She trusted them, didn't she? Lily imagined them chatting up Peter, moving in on the relationship that she had worked so hard to cultivate. It had been impossible for anyone at her agency to even get a meeting with this guy, and now she couldn't get rid of him.

What did it mean that no one was responding to her messages? She considered sneaking downstairs to see if Peter was still there. No, she couldn't do that. If he saw her, she'd be caught in a lie.

"Well," she sighed, "I guess I'll just have to commit."

The Dangerous Woman's Guide To Domesticity

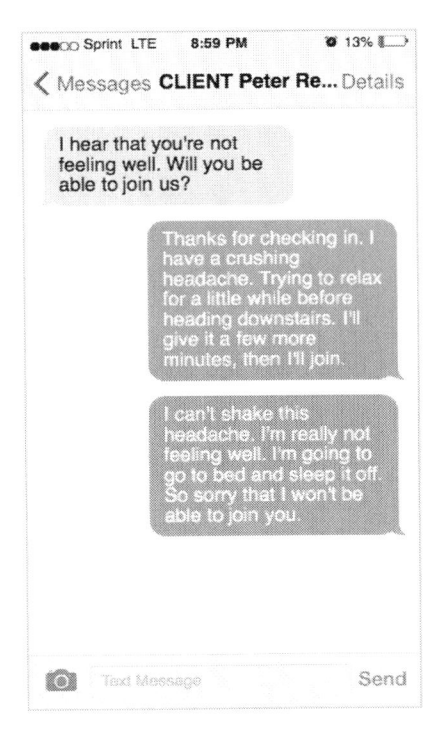

> **Sprint LTE 8:59 PM 13%**
> **< Messages CLIENT Peter Re... Details**
>
> I hear that you're not feeling well. Will you be able to join us?
>
> Thanks for checking in. I have a crushing headache. Trying to relax for a little while before heading downstairs. I'll give it a few more minutes, then I'll join.
>
> I can't shake this headache. I'm really not feeling well. I'm going to go to bed and sleep it off. So sorry that I won't be able to join you.

She turned on the shower. Just as she started to undress, her phone buzzed twice. It was from Valentina:

> **Messages Valentina Cruz**   Details
>
> Peter Reardon is STILL HERE
>
> He's sitting at the bar watching television. Didn't even stop by to say hello to us.

Lily took the phone into the bedroom and fished in her computer bag for her charger. She placed the phone on the bedside table, screen down. Somehow, that seemed to make something better. She returned to the bathroom, finished undressing and stepped under the hot jets of water.

Lily's phone buzzed. She had fallen asleep sitting up in bed, wearing the hotel robe. The TV flickered with the sound of a car chase from an '80s action movie. She reached for the phone:

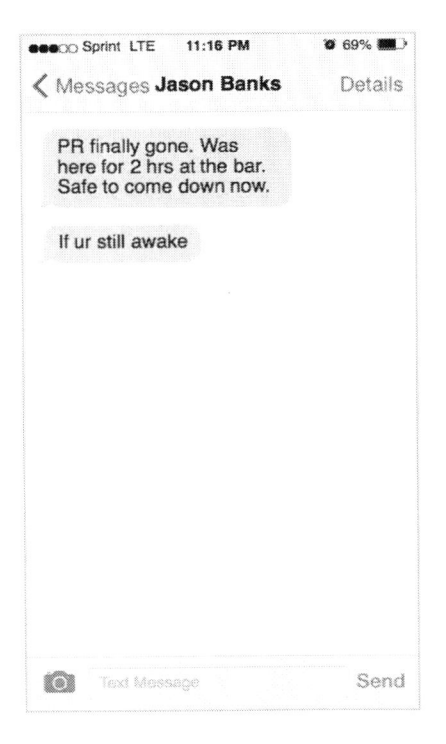

> Sprint LTE 11:16 PM 69%
>
> ‹ Messages **Jason Banks** Details
>
> PR finally gone. Was here for 2 hrs at the bar. Safe to come down now.
>
> If ur still awake

Lily put on her clothes from earlier and met the team downstairs. According to their report, Peter had stayed for two hours. He had asked them about her twice, but refused to join them. Instead, he sat alone at the bar, watching TV, checking his phone and occasionally eyeing the elevator bank. He knew that Lily was avoiding him, and had suspected that she would join the group later, even after she told him she was going to bed.

* * *

"So, what are you going to do about it?"

"What do you mean, 'do'?" Lily was suspicious of this line of questioning from her boss. She had hoped for some help with fending off Peter's increasingly aggressive advances. "He wants me to...engage in some kind of relationship with him that has nothing to do with work."

She wanted to scream, "He wants me to sleep with him!" but it sounded too inappropriate to say out loud.

Her boss pretended to give it some thought. "I get it," he started slowly. "But isn't there something you could do to help things along? To help us get the business? What do you think you can...do about it?"

Lily couldn't believe what he had just said. Clearly, she wouldn't find any help here.

"Should I tell him to leave the money in an envelope next to the bed, or should we just bill him directly?"

Is what she wished she had said.

Lily would turn that event over and over in her mind for years, dreaming up witty or cutting or triumphant zingers that she should have said. She would kick herself for being caught off guard, ashamed at her inability to respond in the moment. It felt like the jerks had won, and all she had done in response was write a tersely-worded resignation letter.

Heck, she had even recommended someone who would replace her. She didn't want to jeopardize the business, after all.

9.2

DRAMA

"YOU'RE SUCH A MADAME BOVARY."

"What did you just say to me?"

"You are a Madame Bovary. All drama."

I took a moment to let it sink in. Here was Julian, one of the most brilliant people I knew, who had just revealed two blind spots: he didn't see why I was so annoyed with him, and he certainly didn't see the irony of what he had just called me. I took a deep breath.

"What makes you say that?" It was my most equanimous tone.

"Well, in my last year of high school, I took this Literature class where we were supposed to be reading Madame Bovary. One of my buddies said something dumb -- I don't remember what -- and the teacher thought it was me, so I got in trouble. I was pissed about it, so I walked out of the class. I didn't want to read that stupid book anyway. I'm a programming guy -- you know that -- and I had already been accepted to the school I wanted. So, yeah, I was beyond pissed that I had gotten in trouble over some bullshit 18th-century Madame Bovary drama."

I was seething.

"Well, I think it's incredibly ironic that *you* would dare call *me* a Madame Bovary, of all things," I started. "That *19th*-century bullshit is actually about a woman who moves with her husband to a provincial town and has a couple of affairs. Her lover actually dumps her. She eventually commits suicide. It was poison, as I recall."

He was silent.

I didn't actually remember the details of the story that well, but I was indignant enough to make my 5-second version believable. I made a mental note to google "Madame Bovary" just to be sure that I wasn't wrong about the poison.

"Yeah. So, for you to call me Madame Bovary is pretty rich."

"Okay, okay; I'm sorry."

It was still a shock to hear him apologize. Since we started seeing each other again, he had apologized more than he had in the three years of the on-again, off-again relationship of our youth. His apologies were appropriate and human. It seemed that my tin man had finally gotten a heart.

But it was his brain that I was concerned about. He had invited me to his birthday party, which seemed completely out of line. Julian had started by telling me all about the preparations his wife had made and about which friends would be there. It would be held at his home, and Jessica had even hired an amazing cover band!

"It was actually Jessica's idea to invite you," he said. His tone was a bit too conspiratorial for my taste. "I talk about you all the time and she knows all about you. Well, not all about you, of course. She knows that you're one of my best friends." His voice softened. "I would really like for you to be there."

"So, what am I supposed to do? Just waltz into your house and act like we're *not* screwing?"

"Well...yeah." He paused. "My kids actually really want to meet you. You should bring your family. All of the kids are about the same age...I know my boys would love to have someone their own age to play with."

"Thank you. Really. But that sounds insane to me." I shook my head, not really believing what I had just heard. "You want our *children* to meet?"

"Yeah, I do. I mean, our kids are going to meet anyway, right?"

I was speechless. Sure, he had talked idly about our future together, but I thought that was just pillow talk. This was entirely too much.

"Listen," I started, slowly. "Even if that were possible, I wouldn't want to disrespect your family's house by showing up there."

"*My* house," he interrupted.

"Your house. And your *wife's* house," I answered. "It's a family celebration. It really isn't appropriate for me to be there."

I was struggling not to scream into the phone at this point. *What the hell? Do I really have to explain myself? Do you seriously not understand why your girlfriend doesn't want to spend all evening with your wife and children in their house?*

I couldn't decide whether he was delusional or just massively selfish. Or maybe he was playing a joke on me -- a cruel, disquieting joke. I didn't see the humor in this conversation at all. It was exhausting. I wanted to put the birthday discussion off until another time. We could talk later, after my objections had had time to sink in.

"Listen, I'm not really ready to talk about this right now."

He wouldn't let it go. "Why not? Let's talk about it now."

"I just need to think about what you're asking me to do. It doesn't feel right, and I'm not really ready to talk about why." I was lying. I knew exactly how I felt about his invitation, and I didn't need to think about anything except why I had gotten involved with a man who was exactly as selfish as I had feared.

"You told me what you think and I told you what I think. That's called a conversation." His voice darkened. "You can't just dismiss me."

"Wait, you think that I'm being dismissive of you?"

"You are. I used to hate it when you did that before, and you're doing it right now. It's my 45th birthday party and I want you there. You just decided that you were going to end the discussion without even bothering to give me an answer."

That was it.

"What the *fuck*, Julian!" I had been driving, so I pulled into the emergency lane so that I could really give it to him. "You can't just decide that you're going to invite me to your wife's house where she's probably killing herself trying to throw you an amazing birthday party, and expect me to come hang out with her and the kids. One of us has to be the adult here and think about the fact that this is fucking bananas! I am seriously worried about why you don't see that."

"Okay, okay." He was backing down.

"And I wasn't being dismissive," I hissed. "I was being as

nice as I fucking could about the fact that what you're asking me to do is insane. Which I believe is the very first thing I said when we started this ridiculous conversation."

I was breathing heavily. My car shuddered on the shoulder of the highway as cars sped past.

My thoughts raced. Julian had hit a nerve with that 'dismissive' accusation. When we were first together, he would accuse me of being dismissive whenever the conversation took a turn that he didn't like. I certainly didn't think I was being dismissive. Actually, I thought he was being extraordinarily selfish. Suddenly, my stomach lurched. Were we back to our old pattern? Maybe we were doomed to this same dance forever.

He broke the silence.

"This is our first fight." He said it tenderly, as if committing the moment to a memory book of our relationship.

I exhaled, then laughed and shook my head. "I was ready for you to say that we're done," I said. I leaned forward and rested my forehead on the steering wheel with a soft thump. My shoulders slumped.

And then came the Madame Bovary comment.

* * *

So, this is what we're calling compromise.

I sat on the edge of the bed, flipping my phone over and over in my hands. My heart thumped in my ears. I inhaled sharply, stood, and made my way to the window. I would not be attending Julian's birthday party, but instead had planned a one-day visit around a client meeting. I had hoped to reset things; to somewhat neutralize the sexual charge that had come to define our relationship. Plus, his birthday was still more than a month away.

I had managed to get Julian to stop sending me nude pictures. I wasn't sure how it had happened, but the nudes had become both exciting and mundane. It was bit like looking at too much porn. As for myself, I was running out of ways to photograph the same old body parts. Julian had overcompensated by pulling back on sending texts at all. At least that's what I had told myself about why he had stopped reaching out to say hello. What I had more trouble explaining, however, was why it often took him hours, sometimes days, to reply to my texts.

"Hey." Julian answered my call on the first ring. It caught me off guard. "I was waiting for you to call."

"Yeah," I said, trying to sound cool. "It's good to talk to you. It's been a really long time. I can't wait to see you."

"Hold on, I'm leaving work now," he said.

I guess he had been waiting for me to call, and was ready to drop what he was doing to meet me. I waited, listening to the rustle and bump as he moved about, then the distinctive thump of a car door closing, sealing out the sounds of the city.

"So, how are you doing? How was your flight?"

"I'm doing really well. The flight was cool. Everything went smoothly. Thanks for asking." I was grateful that he had asked how I was doing. I needed to feel like we were actually friends again.

"So, what are we going to do?" he asked. "I mean, should I book a room?"

"Wait...what?" I was caught off guard.

"Well, I know that you want to go out, which tells me that you don't want me in your room. That's fine. I can book a room for us and we can hang out there, if you want."

I couldn't believe that he had gone right to the sex. Aside from the argument about his birthday party, we had barely talked for months. We hadn't even really texted each other that much. It was like we had crossed an invisible line where Julian only reached out to me when he was feeling aroused. More and more, the exchanges started right in with suggestive messages, then quickly moved on to full-body pictures of him with one hand tucked in his pants, ready to put on a show. I loved seeing him, but I couldn't accept that our relationship had been reduced to dick pics. And to be honest, it was getting kind of boring.

I had hoped to slow things way down when I met him in person. I didn't think it was too much to ask that we just talk like normal people, like friends. I needed to have a sex-less encounter with him so that I could tell myself that I wasn't being used.

"I can't be in a hotel room with you," I protested.

"Why not?"

"It's too much...I just can't be in a room alone with you. Let's just go out and walk around or...something."

This wasn't going the way I had hoped. I didn't feel good about having sex with someone who I hadn't talked to for months. At the same time, I couldn't pretend that I didn't want him. It felt hopeless. I was clearly capable of making bad decisions when it came to Julian. I didn't need a hotel room setup to help me along.

We agreed to find lunch at one of the restaurants nearby. His only obligation was a conference call that he had to attend. Otherwise, we had all afternoon. I'd meet him downstairs once he'd parked his car, and we'd walk around to find a place to eat. I felt relieved. Walking around outside would defuse any sexual tension between us.

I checked and rechecked my hair in the bathroom mirror. I blotted my face with my hands and put on more lip gloss. I didn't want to look too "done." This wasn't going to be a big deal.

My phone buzzed. It was Julian, asking if he could leave his briefcase in my room. It was fine, of course. I texted him my room number.

"On my way up," he said.

I checked my hair one last time and checked my dress. There was a knock on the door. I felt relaxed and genuinely glad to see him. There was no pressure. We were going to go out as friends today.

"Hi," I beamed, opening the door wide. Julian didn't bother to say hello. He looked over my body, then closed his eyes and shook his head, biting his lower lip. I blushed furiously. He stepped inside, dropped his bag just inside the door and stepped to me in what seemed like a single move. He leaned in for a kiss.

"Wait, I can't kiss you," I said. I took half a step backward, already overwhelmed. "I can't..."

He looked at me for a moment, then moved in again for a kiss, wrapping his arms around my waist and sliding his hands down my buttocks. He smelled incredible. His lips grazed mine as I turned away, offering my cheek instead. I could feel his erection rising.

"Okay, okay," he said quietly. "I know that you want to be good. Can we at least hug?"

I nodded my reply, afraid of what I might say if I spoke. He wrapped his arms around my body, holding me close. I rose onto my tiptoes and wrapped my arms around his neck, inhaling his scent. We stayed that way for a long time. It felt like heaven to feel the length of his body against mine. I closed my eyes and hugged him tighter, steadying myself against him. I was losing my balance, but he held me close. I imagined him with his eyes closed, feeling the curves of my body. I let myself go, paying no mind to keeping my balance. He kept my body against his.

I swallowed hard and released my embrace, lowering myself again. Our eyes were locked on one another. I felt that distinctive flutter between my legs. Shoot. My body was refusing to listen to my mind. I couldn't help but smile when Julian stroked my arm. I half turned away, embarrassed by my arousal at a simple touch.

"We should go," I said.

I didn't believe my own words. Every instinct I had commanded me to sleep with him right there. I feinted a step toward the door and he swept his arms around me again. He was gentler this time as he leaned in for a kiss. The world went dark. There was nothing but his lips and his sweet smell.

"Oh my god," I breathed. I slid out of his grasp against everything inside me. I knew that if I kissed him, we'd spend the entire afternoon wrapped in each other. I had to stop things now.

I opened the door and stepped on the other side of it, leaning my back against it to hold it ajar. From the safety of the hallway, I peered back inside. Julian had turned his back toward me. It looked like he was trying to compose himself. That was good. I let my head thump quietly against the door, closed my eyes and tried to gather my own composure.

I peeked around the door at the same time that Julian was on his way out. By chance, his eyes landed directly on my cleavage. It was easy to do. My dress skimmed my figure and dipped low into my decolletage.

"Oh, God," he whispered, looking slightly dismayed.

As we walked down the hallway, I wondered what to do with the tension between us. We stole looks at each other, drinking in each others' profiles and creating sparks anew when our glances met.

When we arrived at the vestibule, there was a man with a stroller waiting for the elevator. Julian and I avoided each other's gaze and waited, the intensity of our arousal emanating from us like a corona. The man glanced at us repeatedly, aware of our energy. The elevator chime sounded and the doors nearest him slid open. He backed in, stroller in tow, and held the door for us. Julian didn't move.

"We can take this one," I offered.

Julian shook his head almost imperceptibly.

"No? Oh, okay." I watched the elevator doors slide shut. We were alone in the vestibule again.

Almost immediately, another elevator opened its doors. I was just starting toward it when Julian intercepted me again, enveloping me with an attempt at a kiss.

"You are making this so *difficult* for me," I said. I had specifically tried not to say that he was making it hard for me. I imagined him replying that it was me who was making it hard for him. This was not time for innuendo.

We stepped onto the elevator and stood opposite each other, grabbing the railing and eyeing each other like two boxers in opposite corners of the ring. Time slowed as we descended. The air between us was thick and hot.

After what felt like an eternity, we stepped off of the elevator and into the light-drenched lobby. The air felt better here.

I felt a little less intoxicated.

"See? See how good and normal we are?" I gave him a sunny smile.

"Yeah," he said, matching my tone. "We're so normal."

* * *

We sat across the booth from one another, feigning interest in our salads. The food was just a diversion.

Julian punched at his salad greens with his fork. "Sooo, the party is coming up. Any chance that you might stay?"

"You know I can't do that." I gave him a gentle smile.

"I know," he said. He looked down at his plate and paused. "I actually thought this trip was, you know, my gift."

I felt heat in my cheeks. "I always want to see you," I started. "It's just that we haven't talked in so long. It's weird to just jump right into having sex with you."

"We're talking right now." His tone was playful, but I sensed a serious undertone. "And the Ritz-Carlton is right there." He nodded toward a building in the office park outside the restaurant window.

I didn't know how to tell him that this felt all wrong. Sex with me was not a gift. I wasn't a professional sex worker, here to give him a birthday freebie. I had come to see him because I really cared about him and had hoped to reconnect.

"Wait a second." Julian stiffened and looked around the restaurant, then scanned the plaza outside. "You're not going to believe this, but this is where Jessica works now. She just started working in one of these office buildings about a month ago."

I resisted the urge to get up and walk away.

"Oh, man. I can't believe I didn't even recognize it." His eyes looked apologetic. "Please don't be mad if I have to say something like, 'This is my friend...' I don't know, I'll have to give you a name, I guess."

I tried to stay cool. This was bound to happen at some point. I just didn't anticipate that it would happen moments after Julian had tried to jump my bones with nary a hello.

"Just so I'm clear, you brought me to a place where your wife and all of her co-workers are nearby. Just walking around, maybe grabbing lunch, oh, I don't know, right *here*."

He nodded, his mouth twisting oddly at the corners.

"And this happened because you actually forgot where your wife works?"

"I guess I was really excited to see you. Call it temporary insanity," he shrugged.

"Nope. Do not blame me for this." I sighed and looked out into the plaza. My stomach churned. "Isn't it time for your call?" I was grateful to change the direction of the conversation, even if it meant that sitting through Julian's conference call.

"It is. I'm so sorry."

"Don't worry about it. I know you left work to spend time with me. It's okay." I needed the time to work through the revelation that I might come face to face with Julian's wife today. It was a wrinkle that I hadn't prepared for.

"It'll take 15 minutes. Maybe 20."

"That's just fine." I gave him a reassuring smile. He smiled back apologetically, then dialed in to the meeting.

I needed to look busy. I picked up my phone and opened the Pinterest app. Morgan's birthday party was coming up in a month, and I had to figure out how to pull off a fashion show birthday party for a bunch of 10-year-olds. She had made clear that she wanted a catwalk and something approximating fashion photographers. It sounded like a lot of work, and I had no idea where to start.

I scrolled through endless photos, saving a few ideas that would work for the party. I saved images of pink carpets, glittery tutus, feather boas, backstage pass invitations, tiered layers of pink cupcakes made to look like a cocktail dress, tulle-wrapped balloons on the backs of white folding chairs, and couture-shop gift bags. It was equally intriguing and overwhelming. It was a bottomless pit of ideas, each frothier than the preceding one, and all better than mine.

Look, there are thousands of ideas better than yours. Thousands of ways to make better decisions than the one you're making now.

Suddenly, I imagined Jessica walking up to our booth. We made quite a pair, with Julian on the phone and me in my fitted dress, cleavage on display.

What's my name?

My heart thumped at the thought. I looked over at Julian, who was listening and mmm-hmm'ing on his call. It had been 35 minutes since he started the call.

My name, what is it? What if I give one name and he gives another? We have to get our story straight.

Julian was animated now, nearly yelling into the phone. I changed my focus, scanning the faces of every woman who walked past. I had googled Julian's wife, and had come across exactly one picture of her. I had studied the contours of her face and tried to plumb the depths of her eyes, hoping to divine what Julian liked about her. There was nothing to be found in her eyes. She was an ordinary woman who had posed for a professional photo, turning her shoulders to the right and her chin to the left for the most flattering angle. Her eyes spoke only of the discomfort of holding an unnatural position. I had nothing.

Scanning every female face was exhausting. I couldn't keep it up. I went back to my phone and opened my go-to mind-numbing game app, hoping to escape my thoughts. The game did its work quickly. It was hypnotic, but did little to relax me. I sighed. I'd have to take what I could get.

I stretched my arms above my head and rolled my shoulders to release the tension that had built up in them. I noticed Julian watching me. Don't leave, he mouthed, giving a small smile. I smiled back in acknowledgement, and went back to my phone.

"What would my name have been?" I asked.

We were walking back to my hotel. I looked up at him, squinting my eyes against the sun's glare.

He looked at me and shook his head slightly. I don't think he knew what I was talking about.

"While you were on the phone, I was really worried that your wife would appear and I'd have to explain myself."

"It doesn't matter. You could have given her any name. I just would have followed your lead," he shrugged.

"You were on the phone, in a meeting. What if I gave her one name and you gave another because you didn't hear what was happening? You were on the phone!" My voice was rising.

"I really don't think it would have mattered," he replied flatly.

Julian tried to screw you in a hotel room after not talking to you for months, carelessly took you to a place near his wife's office and was ready to write you off as a nameless random -- all in the space of a single afternoon. Would he have left an envelope full of money next to the bed if you'd had sex with him?

"Well, I guess I understand," I said in my smoothest voice. "If Aaron were to see us out together, I'd probably tell him that you're just a stray."

I saw a flicker in his eyes. Good. I wanted him to feel some of the pain that I felt. Somehow, after all of the sneaking around we had done, what hurt most was that he didn't have a name for me. I didn't care if it didn't make sense. It didn't feel right.

I was more than a nameless lay. He was more than a stray. But who was I kidding? We'd never be able to fully acknowledge each other. It hurt to admit it to myself.

10.1

FORGETTING

LILY HAD ONCE READ AN ARTICLE ABOUT THE science of forgetting. She was fascinated. For all that scientists had learned about memory, they knew very little about how its opposite function works, or whether we have any power to control it. The article contained a single nugget that intrigued her above all: a technique for forgetting.

"Perfect," Lily had thought, laughing to herself at all of the memories she would love to forget.

She flipped through a mental catalogue of flattened-out memories that she had packed away but had been unable to discard: mistakes, vices, regrets and embarrassments. There was so much to choose from. She was like a kid in a perverted candy store.

She decided to start simple, with something that she could prove to herself that she had forgotten. She would try her hand at "forgetting" dark chocolate Dove ice cream bars. She had been eating too many of them lately. For a while, it had seemed like an inconsequential little vice. But when her jeans started hugging her a bit too tight, she knew it was time to give them up. Unfortunately,

Dove bars were divine. They didn't just taste good; they were a whole sensory experience. If she could forget them, she could forget all kinds of things.

The first step was to disassociate the feeling from the act of eating. Soon, the lush, velvet smear of chocolate so fine that it's melted by her breath; the first bite into the curved hip of the bar; the veil of chocolate on her lips like the lingerings of a French kiss; the snap of the crust and the thrill to the roots of her teeth as they sliced through slow-churned ice cream -- all of those sensations were reduced to clear-eyed facts.

It worked. Now, it was time to forget some bigger things.

Julian was a ghost from her past. His spirit had refused to go quietly to the place where old boyfriends are forgotten. Lily had kept him with her, making love to his memory and letting the rattle of his chains keep her awake at night.

But that memory was tinged with sadness. She remembered the old shame of their first try at a relationship, when she loved him so openly only to be laid bare by his contempt. She remembered tasting another woman's kiss on his lips and pausing, searching his eyes for comfort he would not give, only to have him fling his betrayal in her face after they had made love.

"You knew that I kissed her," he had said. "I could tell that you knew, so why do you have a problem with it now?"

Lily was left unable to breathe; cut so deeply that she hadn't yet begun to bleed. She would be haunted by the persistent shame that she never had the nerve to confront him. Instead, she had only stumbled away from him, blinded by pain.

She had let these memories fade to curves and lines, but they had remained shadowed by a persistent, shapeless grief. Now, she let the sadness fill the curves, giving shape to those old memories again. It crept through her memory like mist, silently billowing over itself and curling under closed doors to passageways long abandoned; pouring through the rusted locks and chilling the air inside.

Now it was she who was the other woman. Would Julian's wife taste her kiss on his lips? When his wife asked who the other woman was, would Julian give her a name? Or would he spin her into some nameless woman who he had banged in a hotel room?

She reframed their relationship through the mist of sadness. She felt its chilly fingers when she waited an hour, or two, or twelve, for a reply to her text message. She tried to push away the thought that he was punishing her. Or maybe, she thought, they had said everything that they had to say to each other. If they weren't going to be together, it was pointless to continue to pine -- right?

Lily thought back to that article and the Dove bars. She had to separate her feelings from her thoughts of Julian. She dredged it up and shaped it into a wedge, a simple tool that she could use to keep them apart.

To use her new tool effectively, she'd have to start small: She would train herself to forget the details that once ruled their little world. She would not look at the time and reflexively think about what he was doing. She would not file away little absurdities she had observed during her day to delight in with him, muffling their late-night giggles. She would try her hardest not to let her eyes flit to the text message indicator, stomach flipping with delight at the thought of even a hello from him.

And so it was that Lily forced the memory of Julian's weight pressed into her, probing her with kisses so urgent that they stifled her breath, to a simple, clear-eyed fact. Yes, they had kissed. That's all. She packed away the warmth spreading deep in her belly; the urgent, pulling sensation as her labia swelled. She pushed aside the moment when he entered her, so hard and so ready that there was no need to guide him in; her need for him so intense that her back arched and head drew back as she exhaled "yesssss" upon his entry. It was perfect. A perfect, incredible fact.

"I will let him go," she said out loud.

The words were like ashes in her mouth. She shut her ears against the sound of them, and instead unfurled her fingers in slow motion, watching her sinews stretch as she articulated the movement to the tips of her fingers. She let her eyes slide shut and concentrated on connecting her thoughts with her body movement. She visualized herself letting go in as many ways as she could imagine: letting a cool slip of ribbon thread through her fingers as a balloon pulled into the sky; feeling the breeze blow unfettered over her skin and swirling around her fingers; uncurling her caged digits to release a butterfly, urging it to take flight with her open palm.

Still, Lily still wasn't ready to go through with the final articulation. Her fingers licked into nothingness for one last taste of Julian.

10.2

POISON

DAY ONE.

I stared at the worksheet on my computer screen. An open cell stared back at me. I had to figure out how to fill the week between Morgan's basketball and soccer camps, and that open cell represented the problem week. Kali would be at a science program in Maryland, so she'd be away for a little more than a month. Inanna would be finishing her last week of drama day camp, then starting a different program at a local teaching farm. She'd learn how to feed and care for the sheep, goats and chickens on the property, and would wrap each afternoon with a pony ride. I had to admit that I was pretty excited about the idea of a daily pony ride. I caught myself smiling, and reminded myself to focus. There had to be some program for Morgan during that week. I had to fill that open cell.

I went back to the calendar on my phone. June 7th loomed. It was only ten days away. It was already getting more and more difficult to keep the girls focused on school. Inanna had made it a habit to remind me how many more days of school were left. Every morning as she got ready for school, and every afternoon when I picked her up, she'd chirp, "Guess what?" It was getting harder and harder to pretend that I didn't know what she was going to say next. And, frankly, I didn't need the pressure. I hadn't finished the patchwork quilt of camps, vacations, playdates and activities that keep the family occupied each summer.

I closed my laptop. Staring at that empty cell wasn't helping at all. I shook my head. It wasn't the worksheet that was bothering me. I was actually distracted by that date. June 7th was also Julian's birthday.

I looked at the calendar on my phone again. All of a sudden, ten days seemed like an eternity. I was ready to end it with him now. I couldn't even remember the last time we had talked. Had it been two weeks, or just one? Three? My perception of time had bent around this relationship, and I was losing my grip on it.

I had tried not talking to him before; deleting him from my contacts and resolving not to respond to his messages. It was useless. My attraction to him was an itch that begged to be scratched. I fretted over whether he even noticed my silence. Time after time, I was reduced to a simpering girl who just wanted to know whether the boy she likes is thinking of her. And whenever he reached out to me first, I found myself feeling spiteful. Finally, *I* could ignore *him*. I wasn't being ignored; I was doing the ignoring. The fact that it made me feel petty didn't stop me from behaving that way. But this time, I told myself, things were different. I was really ready to end the relationship. Even so, it felt like it would be a low blow to break things off right before his birthday.

I sighed. Maybe Julian had called it. Maybe I was, as he had put it, a Madame Bovary.

Please. Madame Bovary never had to piece together a summer schedule for the kids.

I turned my screen off and pushed the phone away from me.

Bovary committed suicide. It was poison, as I recall.

That had been my reply to Julian. Of course, there was no way that I'd swallow poison because of him. My stomach convulsed in a silent sob. I closed my eyes and willed control over my body. Still, the thought of Madame Bovary's demise made me feel miserable.

I had to distract myself from my thoughts.

I grabbed my phone again and opened a browser window. I stared at the blank search bar in the browser window, waiting for a thought to come to mind that I could chase down an Internet rabbit hole.

...A cracked kettle...something about out rhythms for bears....

It was the one fragment that I remembered, badly, from Madame Bovary. My thumbs flew across the phone screen. I had to find the rest of the passage.

> "...The truth is that fullness of soul can sometimes overflow in utter vapidity of language, for none of us can ever express the exact human measure of his needs or his thoughts or his sorrows; and human speech is like a cracked kettle on which we tap crude rhythms for bears to dance to, while we long to make music that will melt the stars."

My breath caught in my chest. It was like sticking my finger into a sore spot and examining the facets of my pain.

Suddenly, I had the beginnings of an idea. I'd say

everything that I hadn't dared to say before. I would tell him that it was for his birthday, and he would believe me. And when it was over, he would know that I had ended it. I would melt the fucking stars.

After a searching for a few more minutes, I found the first quote. It seemed to capture the kind of madness that I felt. I hammered at my keyboard. This was a long one; part of a letter from 19th-century French writer Honore de Balzac to his lover, the countess Evelina Hanska. At the last moment, I decided against attribution.

He can look it up himself, if he even cares.

This was the right thing to do. Probably. I hesitated. Once I sent this message, I wouldn't be able to go back. I'd have to see the plan through to the end. I copied the message into my notes app and decided to give it some time.

* * *

I lay with my back to Aaron and fought the urge to move again. It was useless; I couldn't sleep. I opened my eyes wide against the near-darkness of the bedroom. I wanted to let my eyes adjust before getting out of bed. I thought through my next few moves: I would peel the covers back to avoid letting cold air under the sheets, then unplug my phone and hold its screen against my thigh to block the telltale blue light as it awoke. I'd pad across the room, grab my robe from the closet, slide into it, drop the phone into my pocket and tie the robe before exiting the room. I was sure that I could pull it off without waking Aaron.

I had just finished my escape plan when Aaron stirred. He

turned over and murmured softly, then settled again with his arm thrown over my waist. I held my breath, then waited as his breath slowed and deepened again. He was still sleeping soundly. I counted each time he exhaled. 30 breaths. I lay with him, eyes wide open, counting. His breath was hypnotic, like waves on the shore. I could fall asleep to this. I could, but I wouldn't. I had already decided what I was going to do next.

Ten...eleven...twelve....

Suddenly, I felt the muscles in the ball of my right foot clench and my toes fold involuntarily.

Nonononononooooooo!

I brought my knee to my chest and reached down to my toes to massage them. A shock of pain seared across the bottom of my foot. I jerked my hand away from the pain, then gingerly touched the area with my fingertips. Aaron sat up, arms reaching for me as if I were going to fall out of bed.

"What? What's going on?" He was shaking himself out of what appeared to be a very satisfying slumber.

"Aargh, foot cramp," I groaned.

Aaron peered through the barely-lit room at my foot, blinking and moving his face close to get a better look. He shook his head, then reached toward his bedside table to turn on the lamp.

"No, don't turn on the light," I protested. "Go back to sleep. I'll drink some water and see if I can work the cramp out."

"Okay," he said, adjusting his pillow. "You can have my water." He offered me the half-empty bottle sitting next to his lamp.

"Thank you."

I swung my feet to the floor and stood, keeping most of

my weight on my left foot. I hobbled to the bathroom with Aaron's bottle of water tucked under my arm and my phone in my hand; screen sealed tightly against the side of my thigh.

I sat on a bench in the bathroom and folded my right ankle over my left knee. I could examine my foot more easily by the night light in the bathroom. The cramping had subsided a bit, but my toes were still frozen in their splayed position. My fourth toe had pulled down toward the arch of my foot. It looked...hilarious. I tried to stifle the laugh bubbling in my belly and snorted instead.

"Everything OK?" Aaron's voice sounded distant, tired.

"It's nothing. I mean, it hurts, but..." I snuffled, trying to keep my laughter in check. "Oh my god, my foot looks so crazy. You should see this."

Aaron murmured something and went back to sleep.

I went back to my foot. I hadn't meant to wake Aaron, and I was determined not to do it again. I found the most tender spot with my fingers and pressed. The muscles shot a bolt of pain back in protest. So, that was the right spot. I eased the pressure through the balls of my fingers and kneaded the surrounding area, taking care not to press the most sensitive spot. That felt good. I stopped massaging after a minute and examined my toes. Before my eyes, they froze again, splayed and locked. That fourth toe pulled down again. It was fascinating to watch. I kneaded the area again, this time moving closer and closer to the epicenter. Once I found it, I pressed my thumb into it, hard. I breathed through the pain, and it eventually began to subside. I pressed again, this time massaging back and forth as I applied pressure. The pain soon gave way to discomfort, which I could live with.

I put my foot on the floor and did a few heel raises, stretching the tender area. I grabbed the water and drank deeply while I stretched, then cocked my head and watched my ankle thrust up and down.

The pain's not so bad as long as I'm the one who decides when to dig a thumb into the sore spot.

It was true; not only had I pressed my finger into the most sensitive spot, I had also laughed at my own twisted toes. I didn't have the ability to stop the cramp, but I had bested it, anyway.

Yeah, it's time to send that message to Julian. Time to make a new relationship with that pain.

I grabbed the phone, copied the message from the notes app, pasted it into a text message and sent it to Julian.

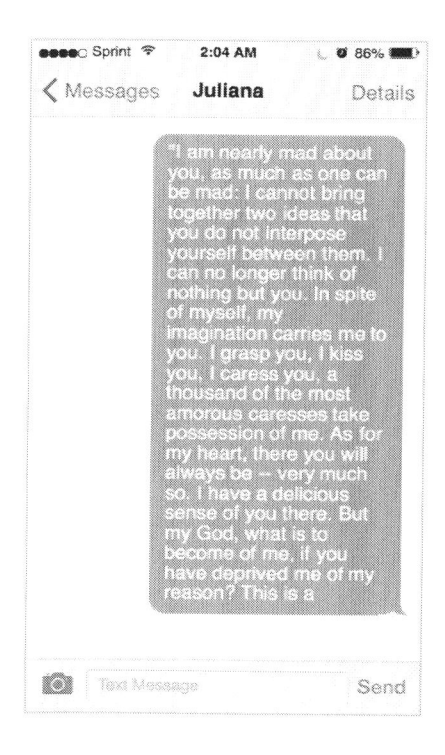

Sprint 2:04 AM 86%

< Messages **Juliana** Details

"I am nearly mad about you, as much as one can be mad: I cannot bring together two ideas that you do not interpose yourself between them. I can no longer think of nothing but you. In spite of myself, my imagination carries me to you. I grasp you, I kiss you, I caress you, a thousand of the most amorous caresses take possession of me. As for my heart, there you will always be — very much so. I have a delicious sense of you there. But my God, what is to become of me, if you have deprived me of my reason? This is a

Text Message | Send

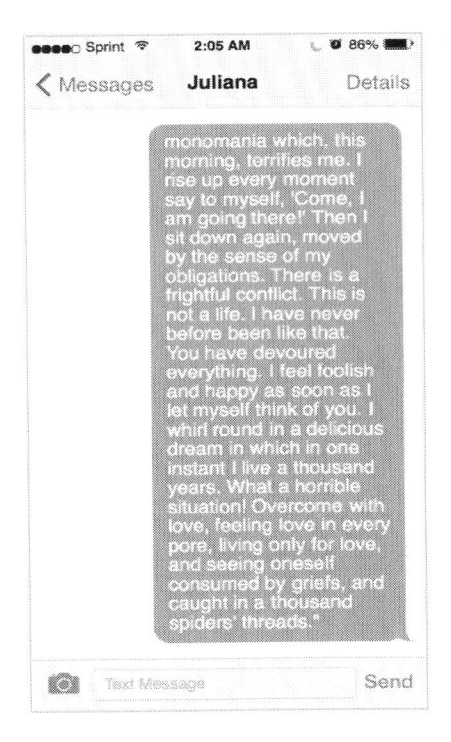

> monomania which, this morning, terrifies me. I rise up every moment say to myself, 'Come, I am going there!' Then I sit down again, moved by the sense of my obligations. There is a frightful conflict. This is not a life. I have never before been like that. You have devoured everything. I feel foolish and happy as soon as I let myself think of you. I whirl round in a delicious dream in which in one instant I live a thousand years. What a horrible situation! Overcome with love, feeling love in every pore, living only for love, and seeing oneself consumed by griefs, and caught in a thousand spiders' threads."

Only after I sent the message did the thought occur to me: What if he actually replies? I hadn't thought about what I would do if he did. I stopped the heel raises and took another drink of water, then went back to massaging my foot with my fingers. It was funny; the more I worked the painful spot, the less the muscles protested.

Suddenly, what I needed to do became brilliantly clear. It was simple: no matter what happened, I would continue to work the tender spot. A reply from Julian was resistance that would need to be worked out. I'd just have to dig my thumb into the worst of it until it went away.

* * *

Day Two.

I awoke the next morning to find that Julian had not disappointed me. There was no reply to my text. I had definitely done the right thing.

I decided to mix things up. Yesterday's message had been from a long, free-form letter. Today's quote would be more succinct; more recognizable. It was a Shakespearean couplet from Hamlet to Ophelia; characteristically powerful in its simplicity. I waited until that evening after the girls went to bed, and sent it.

> **Juliana**
>
> "Doubt thou the stars are fire; Doubt that the sun doth move; Doubt truth to be a liar; But never doubt I love."

Maybe I'd send all of these messages in the evening. He'd have no idea why I was sending them or what to expect, but after a few days, he would know roughly when to expect them. I felt clever. Then, I reminded myself why I was carrying out the plan in the first place.

Stupid, stupid girl. Just send the damned messages.

This time, I knew better than to expect a response. It had been nearly a year since Julian had replied to my messages with anything like urgency. For the last several months, he had even failed that standard. He would reply half a day later, or two days later; sometimes not at all. Then he'd reappear with some idiotic link or joke or some scrap offering from the Internet. He hadn't exactly gone away, but it was impossible to know how to reanimate us.

My messages sliced hot and bold, and were meant to shake him. They were meant to do something to me, too. After all, what kind of fool would send some of the greatest love letters to a man who couldn't even bother to answer? Maybe he had blocked my messages. Or, maybe he was ignoring me. Maybe he had lost his phone! All of this would be for nothing.

Nope; not true. I'm not really doing this for him, anyway. It's for me.

Even so, I wondered if I was giving away too much. Julian's Madame Bovary comment came to me again, unbidden.

He probably thinks I'm being dramatic. The thought stung. *Fuck that. He thinks that I'm a Madame Bovary, so that's exactly what I'll give him. But instead of poison, I choose death by exposure.* It made perfect sense. Emotional overexposure was like relationship suicide.

I thought about why overexposure would work to break a relationship with Julian, but not with Aaron. The answer was simple, I reasoned. Aaron and I had a healthy relationship with deep roots and no rot. That same exposure with Aaron meant life, not death.

* * *

Day Three.

The next excerpt had to be a bit less easy to identify. I had found an E.M. Forster quote from Maurice which captured what love can do for the lovers. It captured the brilliant, shining moment that is love; the magic that elevates two ordinary people to something beautiful. It took my breath away.

> **Juliana**
>
> "Love had caught him out of triviality and...out of bewilderment in order that two imperfect souls might touch perfection."

Something was changing. Maybe it was me. This was beginning to feel therapeutic. I finished my glass of wine and turned the TV off. I was done for the night.

Day Four.

The next day's message was an excerpt of a piece by the great poet Rumi. The entire poem was a meditation on the nature of love, but one a few lines of it had stuck with me. This time, I was excited to send the message and get on with my evening. I was going to the movies with Aaron and the girls, and I wanted to get Julian's message out of the way.

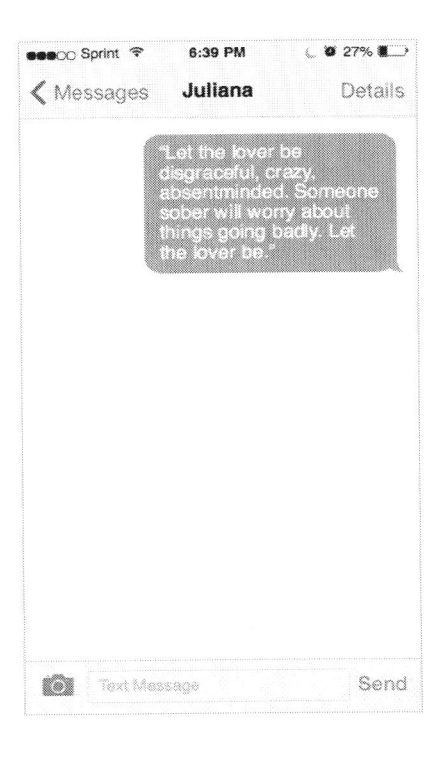

> **Juliana**
>
> "Let the lover be disgraceful, crazy, absentminded. Someone sober will worry about things going badly. Let the lover be."

After the movie, we went out for ice cream. The girls' favorite place was a retro-style soft-serve ice cream stand with benches outside. We laughed and licked our melting ice cream while we watched the cars go by. It was the perfect way to spend a balmy summer evening with the people I loved most.

* * *

Day Five.

I was sure that Julian knew what I was up to by now. He still hadn't responded, which meant that he was ignoring me. Even if he had not checked his messages for a day or two, it was now clear that he was somehow avoiding me. Even in the unlikely scenario that he had lost his phone, he had surely replaced it by now. I halfheartedly wondered why he continued to ignore me. Was he overwhelmed? Overcome? Did he think I was a crazy lady? I thought about stopping. After all, the point wasn't really to bombard him. But I had committed to going all the way. I was going to press my thumb into my pain and manipulate it into submission.

The Dangerous Woman's Guide To Domesticity

> Could I love less, I should be happier now.

I was surprised to find a reply from Julian a couple of hours later.

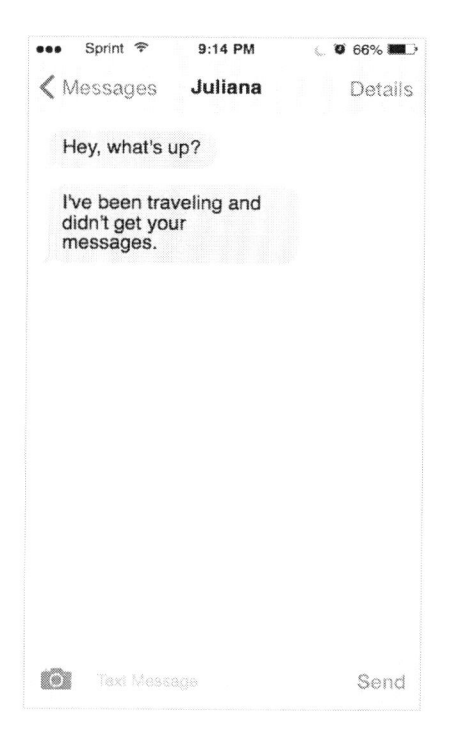

> Hey, what's up?
>
> I've been traveling and didn't get your messages.

Bullshit.

I wondered why he even bothered to lie. Julian used to reply to all of my messages, even when he traveled internationally. I thought about confronting him, but the thought of arguing with Julian made me tired. It wasn't a fight worth winning. I decided to stick to the plan.

I felt a small thrill of victory that he had responded. I decided to remember my shame and let it smother my joy.

* * *

Day Six.

I had Julian's attention. That was good. This next letter was special to me. I had always loved the relationship between

John and Abigail Adams. They were one of those brilliant pairings whose light shines bright even now, more than 200 years after their deaths. They were a formidable intellectual, spiritual and romantic pair, and their love letters offer just a glimpse into their love affair.

Julian and I were no John and Abigail Adams, but there was something in Abigail's yearning for her absent husband; in her support of him from afar while sacrificing her own ability to be with the man she loved; that spoke to me.

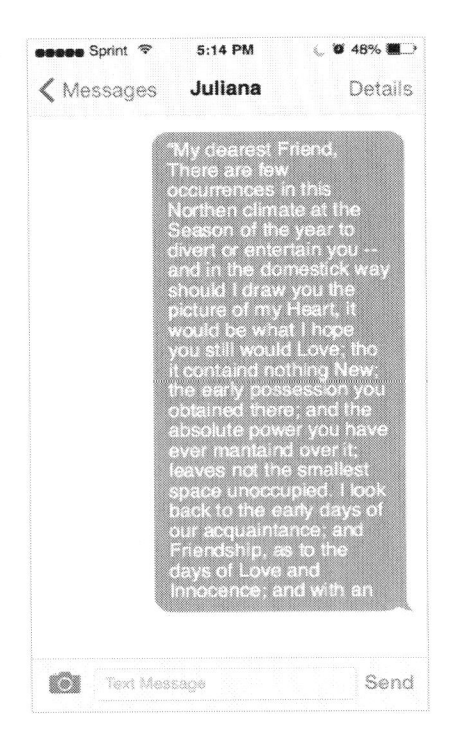

> "My dearest Friend, There are few occurrences in this Northen climate at the Season of the year to divert or entertain you -- and in the domestick way should I draw you the picture of my Heart, it would be what I hope you still would Love; tho it containd nothing New; the early possession you obtained there; and the absolute power you have ever mantaind over it; leaves not the smallest space unoccupied. I look back to the early days of our acquaintance; and Friendship, as to the days of Love and Innocence; and with an

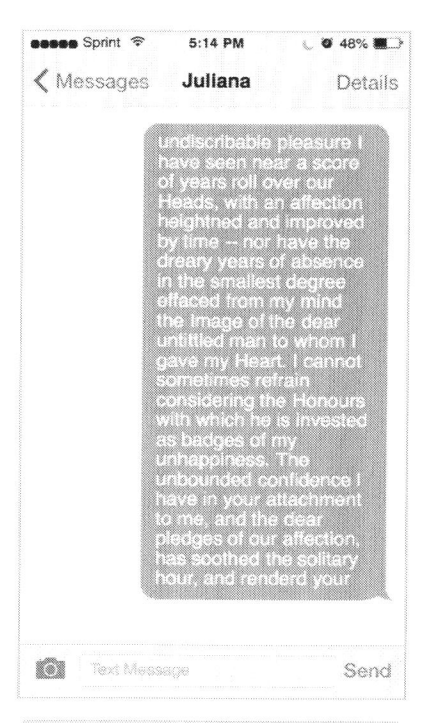

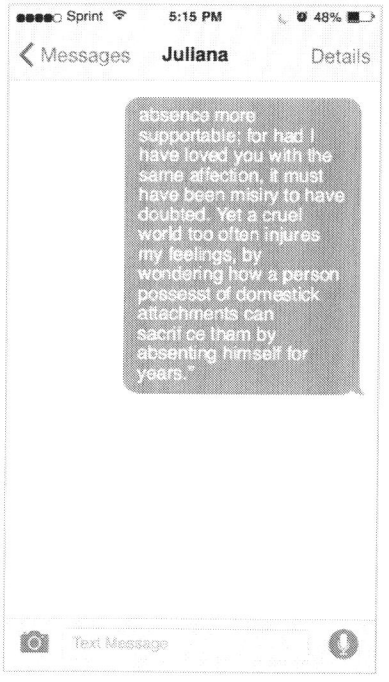

undiscribable pleasure I have seen near a score of years roll over our Heads, with an affection heightned and improved by time — nor have the dreary years of absence in the smallest degree effaced from my mind the image of the dear untittled man to whom I gave my Heart. I cannot sometimes refrain considering the Honours with which he is invested as badges of my unhappiness. The unbounded confidence I have in your attachment to me, and the dear pledges of our affection, has soothed the solitary hour, and renderd your

absence more supportable; for had I have loved you with the same affection, it must have been misiry to have doubted. Yet a cruel world too often injures my feelings, by wondering how a person possesst of domestick attachments can sacrifice them by absenting himself for years."

I had always wondered whether Julian was my second great love. Maybe Kevin was my first and Aaron was my third and final, most enduring great love. Then again, it was possible that I had been wrong about the whole thing. Maybe I didn't have to wonder at all. Kali, Morgan and Inanna were my three great loves. Each of them were of me and yet separate from me; each full of her own potential that echoed back to my own girlhood. My heart surged at the thought.

I closed my eyes, letting the words ring in my head like an incantation: *My darling girls, I wish you a life full of memories and of forgetting and of all the things that make it worth both.*

* * *

Day Seven.

I had found a real gem online. It was a love letter from Elizabeth Taylor to her husband Richard Burton, just days before they split up and months before they finally divorced. This letter crackled with anger and jealousy, but was still held together passionately, morosely, by the helpless feeling of being in love. I could relate. I channeled Liz Taylor:

> "My darling (my still) My husband. I wish I could tell you of my love for you, of my fear, my delight, my pure animal pleasure of you -- (with you) -- my jealousy, my pride, my anger at you, at times.
>
> Most of all my love for you, and whatever love you can dole out to me -- I wish I could write about it but I can't. I can only 'boil and bubble' inside and hope you understand how I really feel.
>
> Anyway I lust thee. Your (still) Wife. P.S. O'Love, let us never take each other for granted again! P.P.S. How about that -- 10 years!?"

* * *

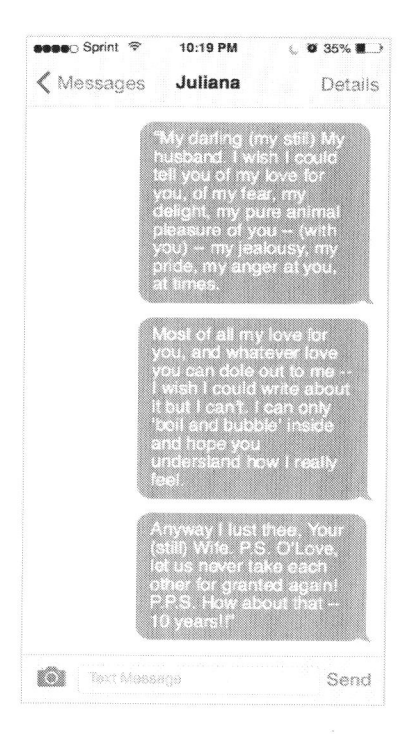

Day Eight.

I was getting tired. And at this point, I was really struggling to find more letters to send to Julian. This was hard. I never imagined that things would be so complicated between us. Back when we were in college, it certainly had not occurred to me that we would end up like this. We were just kids that first time around.

I was a child and he was a child -- Annabel Lee!

My fingers flew as I googled Edgar Allan Poe's poem about two doomed young lovers. This time, I typed the words into my phone to get the line breaks right.

[Screenshot of text message to Juliana:]

"I was a child and she was a child / In this kingdom by the sea / But we loved with a love that was more than love — / I and my Annabel Lee; / With a love that the winged seraphs of heaven / Laughed loud at her and me."

Julian replied almost immediately to this last message. I took note of the words he chose. He didn't ask, "Why are you sending all of these messages?" Maybe he didn't want to convey annoyance. But he could have asked, "What inspired all of these messages?" which would have left it up to me to explain myself in more detail. Instead, he asked, "Why did you send all of these verses?" And the fact that he used the word verses instead of messages or texts seemed to soften the question.

I was pretty sure that the question was genuine, and was rather carefully put. But I was executing my plan, and he had taken days before even bothering to respond. I wasn't going to answer his questions. And all I could think was, *That's cute; he thinks I'm done sending these messages.*

* * *

Day Nine.

Yesterday had been hard, but today's search for a quote or passage or letter was brutal. I struggled for a couple of hours to find passages or letters that really felt meaningful. I cast an even wider net, looking beyond songs and poems and great love letters. I didn't know exactly what I was searching for, but I was sure that I'd know it when I found it. And then, I did.

My search had led me right back to a famous love letter; this time from Oscar Wilde to his lover Lord Alfred Douglas. Wilde was in prison as a result of their relationship, which was deemed "indecent" at the time. And apparently, Douglas was a real jerk. He had abandoned Wilde, leaving him to serve out his prison term without so much as a letter.

Wilde's letter to Douglas was long and ranging, and probed his lover's essential selfishness. But it was the final line that I loved most. It was perfect. So much so, that I didn't bother to put it in quotations.

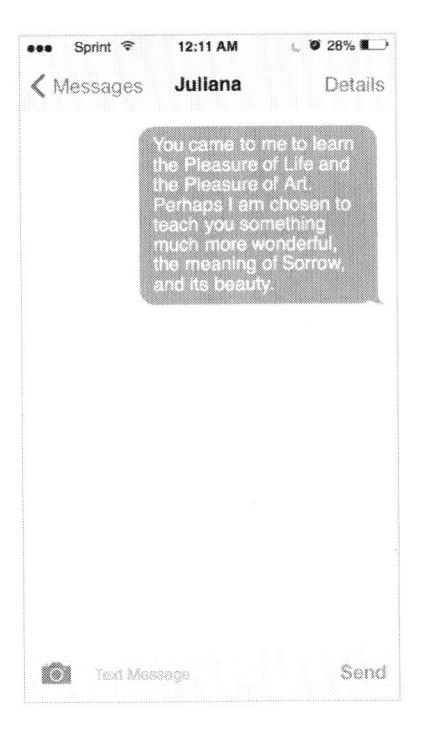

> You came to me to learn the Pleasure of Life and the Pleasure of Art. Perhaps I am chosen to teach you something much more wonderful, the meaning of Sorrow, and its beauty.

I sent the message, then went to bed.

* * *

Day Ten.

The next morning, my phone vibrated with a new message alert. Julian had replied to the message I sent the night before.

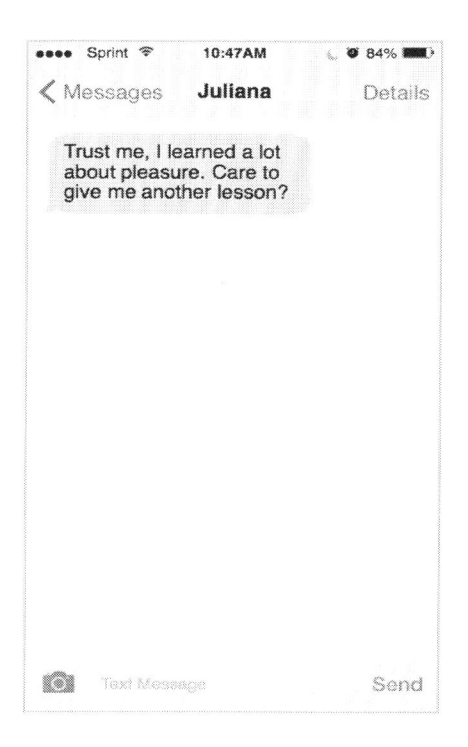

> **Messages** **Juliana** Details
>
> Trust me, I learned a lot about pleasure. Care to give me another lesson?

"Fuck you, Julian," I whispered under my breath. I deleted the message.

This exercise was exhausting. I had planned to send a message per day for each of ten days, but I couldn't find another thing to say to Julian. In that moment, I decided: there simply wouldn't be a tenth message. I was spent.

* * *

For most of the next day, I avoided sending Julian a text. I didn't want to seem overeager. I waited until bedtime to send him a birthday wish.

The Dangerous Woman's Guide To Domesticity

> I wish you another year of fun, excitement and beautiful memories. And today, your special day, I wish you an extra dose of all the things that bring you joy.

> Happy Birthday.

His reply was polite. Delayed, but polite.

> **Juliana**
>
> I wish you another year of fun, excitement and beautiful memories. And today, your special day, I wish you an extra dose of all the things that bring you joy.
>
> Happy Birthday.
>
> Thank you :)

I was finally free.

* * *

I stood at the kitchen island, chopping vegetables. Aaron was reheating the chicken. Tonight's dinner would be a chicken and vegetable stir-fry with noodles. It was a perfect one-dish meal that everyone in the family actually enjoyed. Plus, it helped clear the refrigerator of a few leftovers. Win-win-win.

But the biggest win was that the family was together, and everyone was in a good mood. The girls had finished their last day of school, and Morgan and Inanna had played outside for hours, running off the end-of-school energy that had powered them over the last couple of weeks. Inanna was sitting at the island opposite me, doing her number art. She had given it up for a while, but after discovering a stash of old artwork that I had saved, she decided to take it up again. Today, she was drawing cascading columns of numbers in shades of green and pink. She had gone through a blue period, where the numbers were shot through with the occasional purple or yellow highlight, and a brown period, which was my least favorite series. Green and pink reminded me of springtime and possibilities, and I quietly hoped that she would stay with this colorway for a good, long time.

Kali had hung out with her friends for the afternoon, then come home to spend time with us. I didn't know why, but I knew better than to question our good luck. It was good to have her at home. Kali was on the computer now, playing DJ for the family. She was good, and even threw in an occasional late '90s hip-hop riff for Aaron and me. She kept her selections family-friendly, too, and knew the songs well enough to creatively avoid any bad language. She was really good.

Morgan was laying with her belly on the floor and her feet in the air, swinging her bare feet back and forth. She was propped on her elbows, studying her Guinness' Book Of World Records. It was a kids' dream: a perfect mashup of the trivial, the macabre, the idiotic, the downright disgusting and the truly impressive. Morgan had spent the last 20 minutes enlightening Aaron and me with highlights from the book.

"Oooooooohhhhhh..." Morgan ran into the kitchen, feet slapping on the kitchen floor. "This burger," she said, holding the book aloft with one hand and pointing to a picture with the other, "weighs 1,793 pounds." She paused for emphasis. "It's the biggest burger in the world. The biggest commercially available burger in the world" she said the words "commercially available" slowly.

Inanna paused her cascading number art. "Let me see," she said, and craned her neck to get a look at the burger. Morgan swiveled the book in her younger sister's direction.

" 'Commercially available' means that it's available for someone to buy," Aaron clarified. "A company either made it or sponsored it. That burger was probably made by a restaurant, right?"

"That's the best part." Morgan wiggled her eyebrows and grinned impishly. "It was made by a restaurant right here in Michigan." She gave Inanna a look. "Pleeeeease? Can we go? I want to see the burger!"

"Yeah, we want to see the burger!" Inanna echoed.

Aaron and I exchanged a look. A 1,793-pound burger wasn't his idea of a can't-miss attraction any more than it was mine. I gave him a nod that said, you take this one.

"Yeah, we can go." Aaron's voice matched the girls' enthusiasm. "Let's put it on our travel list. New York, Toronto, Chicago, San Francisco, and the giant burger restaurant." I couldn't believe my ears. "Find out where the restaurant is located," he instructed Morgan.

"Okay, dad. But first..." she was already absorbed in the book again and took a seat next to Inanna at the island, flipping through the pages.

Aaron and I did a surreptitious fist bump.

Morgan soon re-animated. "This says that the oldest woman in the world lived to 122 years old. She was actually 122 years and 164 days old." Her face brightened as she looked at me. "Hey, remember when we heard about that 120-year-old woman on the news, mom?"

"I do," I replied. I glanced up from the onions I was chopping and gave her a small smile.

Inanna wrote the number into her art, somehow tickled by the number sequence. "Look, mom. 122. 1-2-2. Get it?"

"Mmmhmm," I replied.

I did not get it, but I did try to look interested without cutting my fingertip off. I once had a co-worker who chopped off the tip of his finger while cooking. Since then, I had been obsessed with the thought that I might do the same. I wondered if there had been a six year old begging for his attention while she wrote numbers and a 10-year-old feeding him facts on the limits of human longevity while he bobbed his head to a 16-year old's DJ selections. To me, that seemed like the perfect formula for a nipped fingertip. That, and the fact that I couldn't stop checking my phone. I activated the screen with a wet knuckle, checking for a message indicator. There was nothing, of course.

"How long do you think I'm going to live?" asked Morgan

Aaron turned to me and grinned. He gave me a *you take this one* nod.

I scooped the onions that I had chopped from the cutting board to a prep bowl with the broad side of my knife, sliding my finger along its side to release the bits that clung to its surface.

"Well, your great-grandmother on my side lived to be 92. Your great-grandmother on dad's side lived to be 89."

I decided not to mention that one grandfather had died at 72 and the other at 56.

"Well, I plan to live until I'm at least 120," Morgan replied.

She sounded so sure that all I could do was agree. "I love it," I said.

Inanna looked up from her art, encouraged by my response. "Well, I'm going to live until I die," she said.

"What?" Morgan scoffed. "That doesn't make any sense. Of course you're going to live until you die."

I gripped the knife so that I wouldn't drop it and let out a good, long laugh. Inanna's response was perfect. My six-year-old daughter had just revealed the secret to a life well lived.

"Hell yeah," I said, shaking my head and finally coming down from my laugh.

Aaron gave me a strange look. Morgan and Inanna looked confused.

Kali's voice carried in from the living room. "Oh my god, mom," she chided. She walked into the kitchen, laptop in tow, and gave me a stern look. She then jerked her head toward Inanna, widened her eyes and pursed her lips. "Language."

I didn't care. "Me, too, baby doll." I rested both forearms on the island across from Inanna and looked into her clear brown eyes. "I'm going to live until I die."

I held up my hand for a high five and she gave me a good, solid one. Her eyes danced as she grinned back at me.

Made in the USA
Middletown, DE
23 September 2018